IN
SEARCH
of the
LOST
LIGHT

STUART K. KIMBALL

The Author of *"WOW! Shift Happens!*

Cover design by Rich Carnahan (www.publishpros.com)
Author photo by Glyn Cowden (www.glyncowden.flavors.me)

For my brother, Bob

ACKNOWLEDGEMENTS

My thanks to some of the people
who have inspired me along the way:

Mom and Dad

My children -
Cecile, Robert Forrest and Taylor Kimball

My family -
John, Bill and Ann Kimball, and Joanne Kramm

Cathy Hawk (www.getclarity.com), Wilbert Alix
(www.trancedance.com), Merle Tyroler, Caroline Ilderton,
Dr. Mitch Feller, Dr. William Kimball, the Circular
Church congregation, Richard Almes, Jeanne Barreira,
Gaya Mitra, Mike Richmond, Susan Dunn, Byron
Waldman, Judi Murphy, Martha Martin, Harvey Rogers,
Susan Bouder, Rhoda Sterling, Carolyn Rivers, Hillary
Hutchinson, Bert Keller and Sarah Nichols

1

"Dad!" she shouted. "Are you listening to me? Look at me!"

Willy O'Shea's eyes had been fixated on, but not seeing, whatever might have been beyond the window over his daughters shoulder. Slowly, his eyes drifted down, towards her.

Marcie stared at him, a tear slowly coursing down her right cheek as she knelt on the carpet before him.

Softly, almost whispering, she continued. "Dad, we are losing you. Have you actually heard anything I have been saying to you? What is wrong? Are you eating? Don't you even shave anymore? You look awful."

Willy looked carefully at her, trying to mask all the pain he felt.

'How could she know this, see this? I don't want anyone to realize what is happening. How do I even begin to try to explain this?' he slowly thought to himself.

Forcing a smile he didn't feel, Willy slowly replied. "What do you mean?"

"What do I mean? Don't start bullshitting me now, Dad! You always promised you would never do that. Ever! And now you are. Is it me you are trying to convince or yourself?

Damn it Dad! We all love you. What is going on with you? Tell me!"

"Look, honey, I'm OK. I have just been trying to get some things going. When they do, everything will be fine."

"There is absolutely no food in your kitchen, Dad. None! You look like hell. It is summer and it doesn't look like you have been outside in months. What do you weigh now? Do you even care about yourself anymore? Do you sleep at all? Are you spending your days all alone, in this big house, all by yourself? "

"I've been meaning to go to the store. I'm sort of overdue, I guess. I'll go later. I promise."

"What are you going to pay for it with? There's two dollars in your wallet. There's what looks like some bad check notices in the pile of mail you left in the kitchen." Marcie stood, looking down at him. "And the electric company has given you until the day after tomorrow to pay them or they are turning that off. The cell phone is also way overdue. What are you going to do? Tell me your plan, Dad!"

"I'll figure something out, honey. Really. Everything is going to be OK." Willie rose as well. "Would you mind leaving now, Marcie? I have some things I need to do."

Marcie stepped towards Willy, embracing him. "You are so skinny, Dad. You're shaking! When did that start?"

"I'll take care of it. Why don't you call me tomorrow? Ok?"

"Why don't I go to the store right now and buy you some food? I can go and be right back. Do you want to come with me?"

"Marcie, Please Don't! I am fine. I just needed to lose some weight. You go on and have some fun tonight. I will talk with you tomorrow." Willy led her to the door.

"I love you, Marcie."

"I love you too, Dad. You promise you are going to take care of yourself?"

Willy flashed Marcie the peace sign as he closed the door.

He went to the living room, waiting to watch her car head down the street. After he saw her pull away, he hurried into the kitchen to look at the clock.

5:15. He needed to get going.

Every night at 5:00, Willy walked to a nearby convenience store to buy a lottery ticket. Tonight he would buy a Powerball ticket with his last $2. He was certain that this would be the night. He had enough change in his pocket to buy a banana as well. That would be all that he would need for that evenings meal.

Tomorrow, all his problems would be gone. He could start living again, be the man again that he had lost. He would be able to spend more time with Marcie, resume doing things that felt meaningful and productive, and to definitely start playing golf again. Most of all, he could be the father to his sons that he so wanted to be, and he hoped that they also still wanted him to be; he could quit avoiding them , stop feeling that he was an incredible disappointment to them, to do things with them that were fun. They were growing up too quickly, and he did not want to completely miss the next years of their lives.

After again carefully looking both ways out the window to be sure Marcie really was gone and not just parked and watching, Willy went to the kitchen sink and refilled the plastic water bottle he kept there. As long as he took a vitamin every morning, ate a banana or two everyday and drank plenty of water, he was sure that he could keep hanging in there until something financially good happened. He was glad he had lost plenty of weight. Willy had felt overweight for years. Getting some new clothes was the first thing on his to-do list. He stopped in the bathroom for a quick pee and slipped out of the door.

As Willy walked down the street, he looked about him at the grand homes he was passing; each with green, perfectly tended lawns amidst groomed azaleas, dogwoods, live oaks, huge pine trees and camellias. It was the type of upscale neighborhood Willy had always felt at home in. But at that moment, he would have preferred to be just another shadow, slipping along amidst the late afternoon gloom. He had moved to that neighborhood nearly a year earlier, when he had still hoped something was possible. Now he felt as an intruder might, that he was just a passerby in other people's worlds.

Some of his neighbors were also out walking. Willy recognized many of them, and he smiled and waved as he ambled along the shady streets. Living in an upscale neighborhood might have given him something to aspire to, but on this day Willy didn't especially feel inspired by anything he saw. He felt more like an outcast. He couldn't imagine right then what he had been thinking when he moved into a house that was way too big for him for way more money than he should have realized he couldn't afford. He had rationalized then that it was really for his two teenage sons: it was a nice house they would be happy to bring their friends to and hang out.

Was that when the darkness had begun to take over his thoughts? Had it started long before then?

Most of his thoughts these days overwhelmed him with regrets about the past, about all that had gone so terribly wrong these last couple of years.

'How could he really be divorced from Emilie? Why weren't his sons just dropping by to hang out with him, like they once so often had? What would it take for one of his 'old friends' to pick up the phone and call him to say hi and, just maybe, suggest getting together? How could he have lost absolutely all of his money, his home, all of his dreams?'

Marcie's surprise visit had really hurt him. He was deliberately in hiding, desperately wanting for no one he knew to see the extent of his downfall. Her noticing the whiskers was an extra added disaster. He was down to just one razor blade that worked at all, and it was so dull it didn't make a clean shave. Willy had been using it every couple of days. No one saw him, so he thought he could keep that secret, just like everything else.

Willy realized he was walking with his head down, only looking at the road. As an attempt at some inner dignity, he shrugged his shoulders back and looked ahead just in time to realize his neighbor and former long time client,

Mr. Clifford Soames, was directly in front of him, walking an old white terrier in his direction. Willy would have to say hello. He smiled the best he could in greeting. He also realized he was going to need to pee again sometime very soon.

Despite the heat of a late summer afternoon in South Carolina, Mr. Soames, as Willy deferred to him, was dressed as always in dark slacks, a white button down long sleeved shirt and, on this day, a dark blue necktie. His silver hair was precisely combed; his teeth were perfectly white behind a very thin smile.

"Hi Mr. Soames, how are you?" Willy asked, as he began rubbing his nose, hoping to disguise the stubble on his face

"William, it is so good to see you!" the man began with a hint at a smile. "I was just saying to Mrs. Soames the other day how much I miss our meetings. It looks like all your jogging has been good for you. You know, back in my day we had to run everywhere. Nobody had a car or money but off we went on our paper routes and then to school and then to our after school job. Did I ever tell you about when I worked in an aspirin factory? I stood there all afternoon just shaking this old wheelbarrow as the Bayer aspirin tumbled in. It was my job to keep them separated so that they didn't get stuck together. We ran everywhere then. Not like you young people today with all your automobiles. But you look fit and trim. Glad to see it, young man. Keep up the good work! Love to stay and chat some more but Mrs. Soames is expecting me. Stop by anytime so we can talk again."

'Thanks for asking how I was doing' mumbled Willy glumly to himself as he continued on, sipping his water. His stomach was starting to ache again. 'Does anybody have any interest in me at all? I guess not.'

There was a baseball field along the way to the store. Lately, Willy had been making a pit stop there to use the port-o-let. He was peeing frequently due to all the water he was drinking. But, as he finally reached the entrance gate with relief in sight, he found the gate to be locked. 'Holy Crap!!' The ball field stood in the middle of a large, open area completely fenced with no trees whatsoever around the outskirts. A well traveled four lane road passed by right next to the field. Willy looked about him, wondering if he should climb the fence. But too many cars were going by in either direction. A police officer stood in the intersection a hundred yards or so away, directing traffic. Scaling the fence did not seem to be a particularly good idea.

Nearly dizzy from spinning in a quick couple of circles as he tried to decide what to do, Willy dashed across the road, dodging traffic. He had spotted a Dumpster next to the red bricked single story school across the street. He would have to go there.

He did his best to ignore the cars coming into the parking lot as he speed walked across it. 'Must be something happening here tonight,' he absently thought as he made a beeline to the Dumpster. Just as he stepped behind the large trash receptacle, a tall, thin black man appeared before him carrying a trash can. The man eyed Willy with some suspicion while slowly emptying trash into the Dumpster. He put the can down, and leaned against the trash bin, pulling a red bandana slowly from a rear pocket to wipe his forehead and neck.

"Can I help you, Mister?" the man asked, slowly casting his yellowing eyes towards Willy. Willy was speechless for just a moment as he rose up on his toes, pressing his legs together before finally blurting, as if channeling his inner Forrest Gump, "I've gotta pee."

The black man stood. He was wearing a pair of gray neatly pressed shirt and trousers and wore a name patch that read 'Buster.'

"And you thought you could just stop back here and soil the ground behind My Dumpster? You got lots of nerve, mister. But I guess we all got to do whats we gots to do." He sighed. " Follow me."

Gratefully, and feeling like an old bum, Willy followed Buster back through a fence and into the building. The tall man pointed to a door and said Willy could go there, but be quick about it. "Big goings on at the school tonight and I don't have time for the likes of you."

When he was finally out on the street again, walking quickly and feeling totally embarrassed, Willy could feel his body quivering as he continued towards the convenience store. Passing the police officer, Willy was self conscious, wondering if he might be looking a bit like a hobo, so he raised his hand in greeting as if, of course, Willy was a member of that community. The summer blue uniformed officer never looked in his direction. Willy felt invisible, which was comforting but bummed him out even more than he already felt.

The long, familiar sidewalk stretched before him. Old live oaks lined the streets, and as the trees filtered late afternoon sunlight into flickering shadows on the road, Willy felt a bit at peace with himself. He knew the odds of winning even some money in the lottery were impossible, but his situation was at least just as ludicrous. His current situation would have been unthinkable just a few years before. Then he was, he thought, happily married and living the good life. He, his wife and their children lived in their wonderful home near the beach. His business had been doing quite well and his investments were increasing in value almost daily. For the first time in his life, Willy's father had been openly proud of him. Willy had been so happy then. How it could all have so quickly disappeared into a deep abyss still eluded him. Somehow, he would win Emilie back. Somehow, they would all be together again as a family and their lives would resume, only better this time.

But he had to go to the bathroom again and quickened his pace. He was thirsty, his stomach ached, but he couldn't take the chance that even one more drop of water inside him would be the tipping point.

Finally, the sign for the Quik Mart was in sight. He tried to run but the immediate pain in his knee reminded him instantly that his running days were over. He picked up his walking pace, hoping any of the hundreds of passers-by in their cars who might see him would just think he was another guy out getting some late afternoon exercise. He kept the fake smile on his face to advertise that all was fine and good in his world and hoped the same was true for them.

He quickly entered the store, and headed straight for the restroom. But a young woman with short, bleached blonde hair wearing a navy blue blazer and matching skirt was standing in front of the only bathroom door, talking excitedly on her cellphone. Willy stepped in front of her, trying the door, knowing that it was locked and that he was being rude. But he really, seriously had to pee right then and surely the woman would know this and just keep yapping away.

"Excuse me, but what the hell are you doing?" she nearly shouted in Willy's ear.

So embarrassed, and so in need, Willy half turned, looking into her heavily made up eyes, mumbling that he was sorry, he just had to go really badly.

"Well so do I!" she replied, glaring at him. "Didn't you ever learn to hold it?"

He didn't have an idea as to how to respond to that. Willy glanced over at the counter, hoping the girl working there hadn't noticed this. But she had. Luckily it was his friend, Conchita, and she gestured for him to come over. He quickly did, squeezing his legs together, feeling as if his skin must have turned yellow at this point. She smiled and pointed to an Employees Only sign on the door behind the counter, while whispering "Don't leave the seat up" as she handed him a key.

Willy lingered in the bathroom for a few extra minutes, hoping the lady with the cellphone would be long gone when he returned to the counter. There wasn't much else to do while he waited, so he looked at himself in the Quick

Mart's bathroom mirror. Inwardly, he felt gut punched. It was him alright, but more like him back when he was a skinny college kid.. His blue short-sleeve shirt looked way too big for him, and his shorts seemed to be about to fall down despite the extra holes he had gouged out in his belt. Willy's cheekbones looked like a skeletons. His hair was a mess and much grayer than he imagined, as were his whiskers. The worst thing he saw was the look of abject defeat in his eyes, the dark shadows behind his glasses, the utter sadness that seemed to pour through every square inch of him. He turned away from the mirror, trying to ignore what he had just seen. He went to the bathroom one more time.

He wasn't so lucky when he finally emerged, ready to buy the lottery tickets and to go back home. There was a small line of people, and at the end of it, the cellphone still in her hand, was the bleached blonde young woman. He stood behind her.

"Back again, huh. You want to get in front of me and maybe all of these other people too? Just go ahead, since it's you, nobody will care, they will be really honored to have you get in front of them," she sarcastically said to him. "You are so rude," she snapped, looking right through him. "No, not you, it's that asshole street guy I told you about" bleached blondie said into her phone. "Now he's standing in line with me. Ok, later then." She hung up the phone. And then, her back to Willy, she stayed in place as the line moved forward. And then, rather than move forward, she continued to stand right there, motionless, as another person left the counter.

'Now who is the asshole?' Willy started to say, but she was right the first time and he had just enough remaining dignity to accept that, and so he stood where he was, behind her, trying to not breathe in the heavy perfume she must have drenched herself in. Finally, with no one at the counter except Conchita, the woman stepped forward, bought some cigarettes and left the store without a further glance in his direction.

Conchita was laughing as he reached the counter, handing her the key.

"Women!"

She smiled again at Willy. "Some people are just jerks, you know? You wouldn't believe half the stuff I see people doin' in here. You keep your cool, so you an OK guy."

Willy looked down at the name tag pinned to her red 'Quick Mart' polo shirt. "How are you doing, Conchita? "

"Too blessed to be stressed ,amigo. How about you?"

"I've been meaning to ask you, why does your name tag say Escalante?"

"That's my last name. I always say it means excellent, which to me it does. Don't you think so?" she asked, playing with her long black hair, smiling coyly at him.

"Definitely."

He had been coming in pretty regularly and they had always chatted a bit. Willy thought he would like to get to know her better. He liked her way of smiling, and thought she was quite good looking. But not now, not the way his life was.

"Let me guess. You want a Powerball ticket with the Powerball. Am I right?"

Willy smiled. "Do I have a sign on my forehead or something?"

"Here you go." She flipped some of her long dark hair away from her face, still smiling. "You gonna remember your friend Conchita when you win?"

"I better," replied Willy. 'Never know when I might need that employees only key again."

He left with the lottery ticket and a very ripe banana.

He wasn't far down the road home before he had to pee again.

"Jiminy Crimminy" he said out loud as he picked up his pace, hoping to not have to run into Buster again as he hurried back to the house.

Finally, he burst through his door and, again, took care of business. Relieved, he wandered into the kitchen where Willy found a Styrofoam food container on the counter, next to a bunch of bananas, a package of disposable razors and a note from Marcie.

'I love you, Dad. Here's your favorite chicken dinner from The Pig. Grape Juice is in the fridge. Please shave before dining."

Willy stood for a moment, staring in wonder at the container, almost in shock. He wanted to cry, but there were no more tears. All that was left inside him was a hollow, empty feeling.

"Oh my God, I am really in trouble I need some help" he whispered, slowly descending to the floor, holding his knees to his chest."Please God, please help me. Please! I did not want anyone to know about this. Oh God, how can this be happening?? Help me God. I don't know what to do."

2

The telephone ringing in the kitchen woke Willy suddenly the next morning. He hadn't slept well, although the Ambien he took every night had helped. The phone rang again, and the sound burned into him a fear that the end was upon him. It had to be a bill collector, or maybe the landlord. He wasn't sure why the phone still worked; he was way overdue on that bill like all the others.

Then he remembered. This is the day! He pulled on his shorts, shirt, flip flops and was out the door. Luckily, the newspaper was there. "Thank God,' he whispered as he came back in. Willy was shaking. 'This is it!' There could not be yet another day of more disappointment or bad news.

He quickly opened the paper to the page with the lottery results. Then he remembered that the ticket was still in his wallet. He had to run down the long hall to retrieve it from his bedroom. Willy's throat was dry as he glanced at the ticket, and then at the numbers on the page, and then back and forth again.

Not a single number matched. Not even one, let alone at least a few so he could at least win enough to buy another ticket. He stared at the ticket, the paper. He looked at the empty wall before him.

It was over. It was really over, right now, in real time in this huge, empty, rented house. Any chance he might have had for the future was now completely gone.

He slowly walked into his office and sat at his desk. Head in hands, he closed his eyes.

Finally he lifted his head, and sat back in his chair. He turned his laptop computer on, and then opened the inbox for his email. He immediately went into denial about the lottery, that there was no hope for the future and that he knew it was all over for him. Willy could only hope against hope that something good would be found in that inbox, some response to any of the many emails he had been sending out every day for many months.

Willy had been working. His current 'project', as he called it, was to find business for a local digital media company. Every day, he sent out what he hoped were interesting, enticing emails to marketing directors at a wide range of companies throughout the state hoping to find some new business for the digital company he represented and a check for himself. Over the last month or so, few of those emails had been returned. None had indicated any interest. Maybe today would be different. It was all he had left. But, other than junk emails inviting him to spend money on something, no other new emails were there.

He rose from his chair, glancing at the bookshelf behind him. It was filled with row after row of the greatest self-help and inspirational books that he could find. Over the years, he had read them all; some many times. Quite often, he had been able to open any of these books, and inspiration and actionable ideas had poured out of those pages. It frequently seemed that he could open one to the exact passage he needed at that moment. And at this moment, Willy O'Shea desperately needed an idea, a clue, something to guide him away from the edge of the abyss and back towards the light.

He reached forward, his hand landing on one of his all time favorites. He grabbed the book, flipped it open and eagerly looked at the page. All he could see were black letters that made no sense to him. He couldn't see the words, let alone read them and find some comfort or inspiration. He put the book back and tried several others with the same result. He returned them to their place on the shelf and turned back to his computer. At least if he were working and not giving up, maybe something would happen.

"What is that old saying, it doesn't matter how often you get knocked down, what matters is how many times you got back up," he said out loud , shouting, cheering himself. He stood, hoping for excitement. But there was none. Desperately, he looked around the little room. On one of the shelves were a number of mementos to his former success as a financial adviser. There were several photos of him on the wall with prominent people from that industry. He had been so successful for so long, that when the bottom had fallen out so suddenly, he had been unable to comprehend how far he could plummet so quickly.

He looked before him. Framed on the wall was a question, one of the most important questions he had ever asked himself: it always got him motivated. "What lights you up?" The question normally seemed to always bring forth immediate answers to Willy. His family was his primary source of inspiration, of that there was no doubt. But his answers to this question always went way beyond them to places deep within himself. 'What in his work gave him meaning and motivation? What really excited him about what he did and how it helped his clients?'

And now there was nothing, no answers even whispering just beyond his ability to hear them. It was as if at that moment, the final flickering candle in his soul had been blown out. There was no light. There was nothing at all.

Willy started freaking out. He jumped up shrieking, howling in pain and despair. He fell to the floor, rolling, screaming, and thrashing about. His soul was possessed, maybe by demons, with all the anger, despair, frustration that remained within him. He hollered, he wept, he screamed, he moaned. And then he was still. The phone rang and he leaped to his feet, yanking the cord from the wall. His cell phone rang and he turned it off. It didn't matter who was calling; there was nothing left to say to anyone. Not anymore.

He went to his living room and sunk into his old chair. He drank some water and stared at nothing. Then his eyes began to focus on one of the paintings on the wall before him. It was of an elderly black man and a young girl delightedly looking down at a flounder they had caught out in the marsh somewhere. A tear rolled down his cheek, and then another. He had thought of Marcie when he had purchased the piece. He hoped it would freeze a moment in time when she was so young. Back in those days, he had money to spend on such things. Those were the years when his family surrounded him and they shared great, joyous times together, usually outdoors: playing football or baseball, golf, fishing, swimming or just going to the beach. Whatever it was, they did it together.

Now there seemed to be nothing and looking at the picture brought him further into the gloom. He looked about him, only to see picture after picture, each one sorely reminding him of happy days that would never return. He felt the huge house and all its emptiness closing in on him.

"What am I doing living here? What am I doing living?"

Evening finally began. It had been an agonizing afternoon for Willy. At some point he had tried to eat some of the food Marcie had left. But, like the night before, he had very little appetite and had only taken random bites. He stopped drinking water. He had stared for hours at his computer, racing through all of his contact lists, hoping for inspiration. Not a single new idea had occurred to him. He then went back through all of his emails, going even through the old deleted emails in the trash bin, hoping some bell would ring, a light might flicker within. Nothing happened. Finally, he turned on his Facebook page. He had made it a point to not look at it for quite some time because most of the posted photos and stories were of his 'friends' out having a great time. If anything, looking at Facebook had become increasingly depressing for Willy; he felt himself to be at a great distance from the world of his friends that he saw there. But he looked anyway and he found nothing inspiring or helpful there either and turned it off before the dark feelings totally emerged and gathered around him, taking him down deeper into the black pool he knew he could never emerge from.

He stood and thought about going for a long walk, but it was still ridiculously hot outside and he couldn't imagine stepping out into it. He sat back down in his chair, stared at the wall, feeling nothing, only seeing the mental image of himself as a homeless person, wandering the streets, begging for loose change.

That thought terrified him more than anything he could imagine.

Willy had begun to be aware that insects were beginning to make night sounds outdoors. He stared for a while at his cellphone, which he had turned off in the morning, afraid of who might have called and what they might have said. He wasn't even sure if it still worked. That was another way overdue bill. The land line phone in the kitchen had been disconnected earlier that day, so at least he did not have to worry about that anymore. 'One less thing' as Forrest Gump might have said.

Willy's stomach ached. His soul was beating itself with hammers from every direction. He was a total and complete failure. There was no chance for Willy to pick up all of the pieces of his badly shattered life. What would his sons think if they saw him now? How would his parents respond if they knew? Earlier that afternoon, he had hidden in a back closet when he heard a car pull into the driveway. Marcie had come by, and had come into the house, calling and looking for him. He was glad she hadn't found him shaking and shriveling behind some old clothes, crouched into a tight fetal ball. How could Willy ever face her again? How could he look his sons in the eye? His parents had called, but he hadn't spoken with them either. The shame and disappointment had become too much for Willy to handle.

As the evening wore on, he didn't bother to turn on a light. The darkness brought relief; he only had to hide from himself. But the day was ending, which meant tomorrow would be a new day. He couldn't face another day like this, couldn't go on trying and trying and having less than nothing to show for it. It really was over. He could feel the darkness that he had thought was just the shadow of his sadness rapidly becoming a deep black pool all around him, swallowing him.

'God, I really am in so much trouble right now. Please, please help me."

The room was eerily quiet. Willy wasn't sure that he was even breathing. He hoped he wasn't. The darkness enveloped him. He slid from his chair to the floor, curling up as tightly as he could, his brain painfully banging all over in shame, despair, and frustration.

And then it all stopped.

Willy rose and slowly walked down the hall to his bedroom and found his way into the bathroom. He quickly turned the light on and found his Ambien prescription bottle. There were 4 tablets left. Usually a half of one was enough to put him to sleep. He put the bottle in his pocket and quickly turned out the light

He walked back down the hall, and continued through the kitchen into the garage, where he turned on the overhead light. He easily found a box he knew was full of old sheets and towels. He dragged the box to the windows and sealed them as well as he could with the towels. He sealed the garage door with the sheets. He turned the overhead light off. He climbed into his old Honda Accord and turned the ignition on. He opened the prescription bottle and swallowed the 4 Ambien with some water. He lowered the car windows. And then he sat, staring at the garage doors, listening to the motor running, beginning to smell the exhaust fumes as they began to fill the air in the sealed up garage. Soon thereafter, his eyes began to droop and Willy was asleep.

3

It was hours later. The garage was dark. The only sound was the car engine running smoothly.

Suddenly, Willy was wide awake and alert. He sat for a moment staring straight ahead, not sure what he was looking at. Then he saw the red brake light lit up on the dashboard, could hear and feel the engine running and a horrible smell was in his nose. Then he remembered all of it. Instantly, he turned the ignition off and threw open the car door. He raced to the garage's side door and stumbled through it. His shirt, shorts and socks were completely soaked with perspiration. He looked up into the darkness and could see stars.

'What in the hell?'

Was he alive? Was he a ghost? He couldn't tell.

He walked around to the front of the garage and lifted the door. The sheets were still there. How was he?

He went back into the house and then down the hall to his bedroom. Without turning the lights on, he began stripping his soggy clothing off, dropping them to the floor as he went into the bathroom. He started the shower and leaned his head against the wall while he waited for the warm water to come on. He was shaking, extremely cold, and trying very hard to blot out the memory of waking up in the car. It just couldn't be that he was here, back in the house. He slapped his thigh and it stung. He slapped both thighs even harder and that hurt. With a great weariness, he knew he must be still alive. He stepped into the dark shower, cleansed himself as thoroughly as he could, and began to feel extremely dizzy. He turned the water off, quickly dried himself and fell onto his bed, asleep instantly.

4

"Oh no, I'm still alive!" blurted Willy, looking wildly around his bedroom as he awakened the following day.

Slowly, he sat up and looked around him. By the light coming through the windows, he could see that it was late morning. On the floor near the bathroom, he saw the pile of soaked clothes from the night before. Even with his poor sense of smell, there was an unmistakably noxious aroma in his nose. But his eyes seemed to be working. He didn't notice any weird looking things on his skin.

Willy started screaming, flailing about on the bed. He tried punching himself with his fists but was doing more damage to his shoulders than to any other part of his body.

"What in the flip do I do now? What do I do? What do I do? I can't even kill myself! God, why are you doing this to me?"

He jumped from the bed and ran down the hall to the kitchen. He grabbed his sharpest knife, raised it and plunged it towards his left wrist. The tip of the blade bounced off his skin. Incredulous, he tried again, with the same result.

"What in the hell ???"

He sunk to the tile floor, oblivious to the cold. He started shaking violently, and began sobbing, his body lurching all around the floor in a full length spasm.

And then it was as if a huge veil had lifted, pulling him up to a sitting position. He rested his right arm on his raised knee and looked up through the kitchen window to a deep blue sky.

'Screw it,' he thought, rising to his feet. 'I have to get out of here.'

He went back to the bedroom, dressed quickly into dry clothes and went out the front door. Then stopped, came back in and grabbed his sunglasses and a bottle of water and re-closed the door.

He started walking. He had no idea where he was going, but he was on his way. It was broiling hot, but Willy didn't care about that. It felt good to be moving, seeing the day, the trees and bushes in summer's abundance all about him. Lawns were being sprinkled, birds were flying overhead and he heard the sounds of children playing.

'I am still here, I guess. Ghosts can't sleep and I am pretty sure I woke up. What time is it?' He looked at the sky and the sun and could see it must have been around noon.

"OK, God. I am not dead. Now what?"

And a voice answered. "You already have everything you need."

"What?" Willy turned around, and turned again, expecting to see someone walking close by. There was no one. "What?"

He could only hear the sounds of the neighborhood. But the words rang through him. 'You already have everything you need? What are you talking about? Have I now officially lost it? Should I go home before someone has me hauled away?'

There was no way he was going back to the house anytime soon. So he continued walking, sipping some water, feeling a bit lighter inside. It felt good to be moving, he knew that.

'I already have everything I need? Sure. A completely empty wallet, no food, no prospects, and I can't kill myself. Who wouldn't want all those things? I'm sure a line is forming somewhere to start the bidding.'

Willy walked for quite awhile, despite the heat. Then he began to feel very tired and, suddenly extremely hungry, which was more than unusual. He hadn't even thought about food, much less felt hungry in days, probably longer. He remembered then that Marcie's food was in the refrigerator back at the house. Willy picked up his pace and returned home.

After eating as much of the food as possible, he pushed the Styrofoam box away from him. There was still plenty left over; a breast, some of the rice and beans. He could save that for later. After returning the box to the refrigerator, Willy took an extra long swallow of the grape juice Marcie had left, letting it slowly wash down his throat. The sensation felt miraculous to him. He savored it as he walked back to his office, planning to turn on his computer to see what, if anything, might be new in his inbox. He noticed that one of the books he had looked at the day before, 'Think and Grow Rich' by Napoleon Hill, was sticking a bit out from the others. It was the first self-help type book he had ever read, and it had so often been very helpful to him.

That book had offered him nothing the day before, but he opened it anyway, just to see what he might see. Something fluttered out of the book as he was sitting down and he reached for it. It was a $20 bill. Holding it in his hand, he was completely astonished. "Where in the world... ?"And then it dawned on him. For many years, back in the days when he had some money, Willy had been in the habit of occasionally stashing extra cash in his books. He began to smile. He had $20 in his hand. $20! He briefly searched some of the other books, but he didn't find any more cash. He could barely believe it. He had $20! It seemed a fortune to him right then. He could get some food at the store-food!-and have plenty left over.

Willy was suddenly excited. What a strange day it had been so far. He was supposed to be dead out in the garage right now. But he wasn't dead, he didn't think, so he slapped himself again and it hurt. That felt good. He jumped to his feet and did a bit of a dance before getting very dizzy and sitting back down. He took a long swallow of water and tried to get his thoughts together.

Reality hit rather quickly. '$20. Big deal. In three days I will be right where I was a few minutes ago. And how am I going to sleep tonight and what about the electricity and rent and gasoline and my cell phone bill and everything else?? Flip.'

But he had $20. He turned to his computer. There was something new in the inbox.

It was a reply to one of his emails, one sent weeks before to Ed Shields, the owner of AmSouth Manufacturing. He began reading it.

"Willy-Thanks for your email. Sorry I have been delayed in getting back to you, but my family and I have been on vacation.

"The new product under development that we discussed last year is now finished and we are eager to bring it to the market place. We are ready for your team to create all of the digital media work that we need to present this to our customers. We are prepared to move forward with the media project. I can meet with you next week, if that would be convenient for you. Please call so we can set up an appointment.

Sincerely, Ed"

Willy stared in utter amazement at the computer screen. He re-read Ed's message. Yes they had discussed a project and Ed had said it would have to be at mid-year. 'Holy Smokeronees! New business! There will be money coming soon! I can't believe it'

Rather than phoning, Willy replied to the email, suggesting they meet at Ed's office the following Tuesday morning at 10AM, if that was convenient

Willy was suddenly exhausted. This had been a pretty wild day so far .He went into the living room to lie down for a few minutes. As he lay there, he realized he better get a grip on some sort of reality plan, like right then. 'Great! Something terrific was maybe about to happen. But not today. He had just seriously tried to kill himself. That was not exactly normal behavior. He had tons of bills which included the electricity, rent and his cell phone, all of which were well past due. And he was alone. Incredibly alone and knew this could not be a good thing either.

And at that moment, Willy again heard the voice.

"You already have everything you need."

"Ok, and what would that be?" snapped Willy automatically. But he had $20 now, stashed safely in his wallet. He had an email from a guy saying he was ready to do business.

"What is going on? Did I die and pass on to a parallel universe? Is this real?"

He turned his cell phone back on and, luckily, it was still in service. He thought for a moment and placed a call to his personal physician, Dr. Mike McDonald. He got Mike's nurse on the line and told her that he absolutely needed to see Dr. McDonald that afternoon. It was an emergency that he would explain only to Mike. She paused for a moment and said, "OK-He will see you at 5." Willy then called a therapist he had seen in the past, Dr. Julie Bright. He was somewhat friends with her and left a message that he needed to speak with her as soon as possible. He hoped the phone would still be working if she called back. Then he made the hardest call. It was to Buddy, an old friend who he had known for decades. Buddy had said several times that if things really got bad for him, Buddy and his wife had a guest room he could always use. Willy called Buddy, leaving him a message as well. He needed to get out of this house as soon as he could.

5

Willy sat on the table in Dr. Mike's examination room later that afternoon. The nurse had already been in to take his blood pressure and other vital information. Willy turned the lights off in the room. He didn't think Mike would mind. They had once been neighbors and had known each other for many years. Willy's eyes were feeling very tired, and the afternoon sunlight pretty much filled the room anyway. Willy grew restless as he waited and lifted his head, looking at a full length mirror on the door before him. He just hated the image looking back at him. He thought he looked even worse than he had just a few days before. His neck resembled an ostrich's as it stuck out of the huge white short sleeved shirt he was wearing. Willy was again amazed at how thin he looked. Fortunately, he had been able to at least shave and take an extra shower before leaving the house, but his cheek bones protruded so much that he hoped they didn't pop through his skin. He raised his arm, flexing his bicep, but didn't see much of a difference. 'This is really pathetic' he thought of the reflection in the mirror.

The door opened and Dr. Mike McDonald cheerfully entered the room. Dr Mike's blond, surfer hair framed his tanned, smiling face. Under his white physicians jacket he wore an orange Hawaiian shirt.

"Willy, it is so good to see you today!" he exclaimed. "What's going on?" he asked, suddenly quite serious and concerned as he slowly sat in a chair next to the table, his eyes not leaving Willy's, except to quickly look him over.

Willy began to cry. He was surprised at this, hadn't expected this obvious a question from an old friend would result in this. He had been holding on harder than he knew. He blurted it all out to Mike, leaving little unsaid.

Mike stood and stepped next to Willy, reached his arms around him and gave him a big hug that lasted a moment or so.

"I am so glad you are here right now, my friend. That is a lot to deal with. You are safe now. It's therapeutic to talk about this. The way you felt about all that happened was at least a healthy reaction, although your final response to it was, shall we say, extreme. It sounds like you were under a great deal of anxiety for a very long time, which often leads directly to depression. I can help you some today. Have you made any other calls? Are you going to see a therapist or someone?"

Willy nodded that he was.

"How do you think you got out of the car, Willy? That should have worked, what you tried. What do you believe happened?"

"I don't really know. I am still pretty much in shock over the whole thing."

"Something got you out of there, my friend. Those things don't just happen. You need to give that some thought. You OK now? Going to do this again? Do you still want to hurt yourself?"

"No, absolutely not," promised Willy as he looked directly into Dr. Mike's eyes."I didn't want to hurt myself, Mike. I just wanted to not exist anymore.

"Alright, let me take a closer look at you."

For the next few moments, Dr. Mike gave Willy a quick but thorough examination.

"Willy, here's what I can do for you today. I am going to get you some more Ambien, just enough for tonight, along with some eye drops and antibiotics that you should start using right away .We can't be too careful right now. The exhaust fumes from your car worry me, so we need to be watchful for any possible after affects. I want you to get some food with your $20. I also want you to come back tomorrow for some blood work. You seem surprisingly fine except that, if you don't mind me saying to my old friend, you look like shit. 169 lbs is not enough weight for a man of your height and frame. So eat. And eat right. Don't worry about the bill for this visit. We will work that out later. OK?"

"Thank you Mike" was the best Willy could say, overcome with emotions he wasn't used to. "You don't know what this means to me."

"Actually I do, Willy. Look, almost everyone has some pretty difficult stretches in their lives. It is part of the life experience. Yours is maybe a bit extreme, maybe not. At least you weren't just accepting where you were. That means you do care about yourself. But it is what is happening with you right now and you have taken the right couple of first steps. It's up to you to take the next ones. Think about what that voice said. 'You already have everything you need.' So, you're alright for now and will come back tomorrow? Carol will take care of the blood work. I am also giving you some samples of a medication called Effexor. I want you to start on that tomorrow when you get up. It will help the anxiety and depression, or at least it should. It takes a few weeks before it takes full effect. I think your life going forward is going to be amazing, Willy. I really do. We have known each other for a long time. I know you are a good man. It is easy for me to say this, I know, but you need to look to the future. Your children need you to do that. You are their Dad and they love you. You do your part and it will all work out. Your life going forward will probably be much better than you could possibly imagine right now. OK?"

6

Willy stopped at the Publix grocery store on the way back home. As he walked towards the building, a number of people were passing by him with their groceries, but no one seemed to notice him.

'Am I invisible? Not here at all? Am I a ghost?'

Willy was feeling very tired and a sense of anxiety was rapidly overtaking him as he entered the store. He really wanted to just go home and lie down, to be hidden from the world, but he knew he should eat something. He had promised Mike he would. He kept his sunglasses on, knowing the lights inside would be too bright for his beleaguered eyes.

There were many food items on display just inside the entrance, including stacks of various canned vegetables. He picked his way through them. He could smell something delicious in the air and his stomach rumbled loudly in its version of 'the call of the wild' in response. He remembered that at a nearby counter, a store employee prepared mouthwatering meals using ingredients readily available for purchase. The store handed out small portions of those meals, smartly thinking that most people wouldn't want just a bite of that great food, and would buy the ingredients and go home to cook them up. Willy went to the counter area and saw a small line of people waiting their turn for a sample. He took the place at the end of the line. But as he inched closer to the counter, in the distance he could see a woman he had briefly dated, Allison Maloney. She was over in the nearby fruits and vegetables department and Willy definitely didn't want Allison to see him.

Several months after Emilie had moved out, Willy had met Allison and they had seen quite a lot of each other for several months. But one night, Willy had been feeling pretty low and Allison had assumed it had to do with her. She had angrily lashed out at Willy and he had responded in kind, before abruptly leaving her house. He hadn't seen Allison since and especially didn't want her to see him on this day, not the way he looked and felt. Panicked, he turned to start to walk away from the line, hoping to slink away. But in his haste, he didn't notice a display of canned peas on sale right next to him and he stumbled over it, falling as cans of peas banged loudly on the floor around him. Willy's funny bone hit the floor first. He didn't laugh, but the intense pain convinced him that he was very definitely still alive. The people in line gasped loudly and began to gather around him, anxious for his well being. Allison was among them. Their eyes met briefly. Willy felt so ridiculous lying there, emaciated, starving, thirsty, completely wiped out, embarrassed as he could be lying there in the middle of the peas. And then Allison was gone. As he lay sprawled out amongst the cans, the crowd began to dissipate. A young Publix employee came over and helped him to his feet, assuring Willy it was no problem and he would get the display back up.

"Thanks for being a Publix shopper," the young guy smiled at Willy.

Willy was tempted to leave the store immediately but, with as much dignity as possible, resumed his shopping. After all, he had $10 to spend here. What should he get? He settled on a piece of chicken, a sweet potato and some broccoli, a can of soup, a bit of coffee, and a few bananas. As he stood in line to pay, he was feeling very weak, just zapped. It was all Willy could do to keep standing. He was also sure that people were looking at him and wondering what he was doing there.

He finally made it back to his Honda. As he started it up, he glanced at his fuel gauge. There was just under a quarter of a tank.. He turned the radio on as he finally headed home. Bob Dylan was just starting to sing 'Like a Rolling Stone'. Willy cranked up the volume, loving the song and the music and that he was there to listen to it as he drove along. And then the radio station followed that song with John Lennon performing 'Starting Over.'

Miraculously, his cell phone rang. His friend Buddy was calling to say, sure, they would be glad for Willy to come stay with them for a while. When would he like to move in?

7

Willy went to see Dr. Julie Bright the following morning. As he entered the therapists greeting area, he immediately felt a physical sense of relief; the tension in his shoulders relaxed, his dull headache abated, his nerves felt calmer. He could faintly hear bubbling water sounds as he looked about him at the soothing pale blue walls, a soft red sofa and matching chairs. An oriental carpet blended those colors. On the wall were some photographs of mountain pastures as well as a framed quotation. This one was from Rumi, and it read: 'There is a candle in your heart, ready to be kindled. There is a void in your soul, ready to be filled. You feel it, don't you?' Willy read it twice, and knew he was in the right place.

Julie Bright glided into the room, wearing a long aqua colored dress under her thick brown hair. Her sparkling blue eyes shined in greeting, a red prayer shawl covered her shoulders, a long silver necklace holding a black, oblong stone hung from her neck.

"Good morning my friend, it is so good to see you," she began, in her distinctive southern accent. "Can I get you some water or anything? I don't believe you have been to this office, have you? I'm very glad you called me and are here this morning, Willy! Please, let's go into my session room. "

Willy looked quickly about as he entered the room, noticing it had many windows, each covered in a pale red fabric. The room's walls were a soothing purple and the lighting was subdued. Somewhere in the room, some water seemed to be gurgling over some rocks. It was a place of calming tranquility. Willy sat in a large and very comfortable red chair. Julie took a seat across from him, smiling encouragingly to him.

"What's been going on these past few days, Willy? You seemed extremely stressed out when we spoke on the phone. You have lost a good bit of weight since the last time I saw you."

He told her the whole story. She listened closely, her eyes moving slowly from his eyes, to his hands and feet and back again as he spoke. Finally, exhausted, he finished.

"Wow, Willy. You have had a terrifying experience. Not just last evening, but for all these months. Thank you for sharing it. I could feel your confusion and pain. Clearly, you had a serious breakdown of some kind the other night. It may not be over. If you feel that coming on again, you should not hesitate to call me right away, 24/7, so you won't be alone with it. OK? You are going to need to rest a bit. You must eat some good healthy food. Beginning to exercise again would be extremely beneficial. Going to stay for awhile with your friend sounds like your best option right now. This is not a time when you should be alone. You did real good calling him. You are taking care of yourself. You also did real good calling Mike and me."

"Let me start by giving you my feedback on what I just heard. We have known each other for quite a while, ever since your separation from Emilie. So I am going to give you a lot to think about all at once. You kept saying how ashamed and embarrassed you are. That sounds to me like you are more concerned with someone else's expectations for you than your own. What do you expect from yourself, Willy? Why do you have those expectations? What could you have done differently than what you did?"

Willy could only look at Julie. He had no answers for these questions; his only response was that each one stabbed him in his heart.

"I really don't know other than to say I've let a lot of people down. I'm supposed to be the breadwinner, the man with the plan, Mr. Success. I haven't been any of those guys."

"What kind of success do you expect from yourself, Willy? Describe for me what success means to you."

"I used to be able to answer that, I guess. Now I really don't know."

"Several things come to mind Willy. It could be that you have actually been running from something for a very long time and it finally caught up with you. An analogy would be that you have been pushing a truly gigantic boulder very slowly up a mountain. The mountain keeps getting steeper and steeper. From time to time, that boulder has gotten away from you and you have chased after it back down the mountain, only to start pushing it back up again. Inevitably, you are getting more and more tired and the boulder just gets heavier. So, if that is true, you have a choice. We can spend lots of time trying to identify that boulder, or we can see how we can get you moving in a new direction. Which sounds better to you? We all have our boulders, you know. We have to figure out when to stop pushing them uphill, and to just let them go. Some big shift has to happen for there to be real change."

'So, shift happens?"

"What did you say, shift happens? Omigosh Willy, that is an amazing action phrase. Where did you get that?"

"I just said it differently than you did."

"Well it's really good, Willy. It tells me you were listening and that your mind is working, which is not easy to do when you are under a great deal of stress and anxiety. You should write that one down. Maybe make that your mantra. Shift happens! Wow. I love it.

"Think about this with me for a moment, Willy. The really, really good news is that you are still here. You have the ultimate second chance. It could be a great blessing or just an interruption. You have to decide right now, Willy, which it is. So tell me, what do you want it to be?"

Willy was quiet for a moment. "It is a blessing, Julie. I was just thinking about Marcie, Emilie being my ex-wife, my boys. How happy we all once were. I don't know how I got out of that car, why I was so awake, moving so quickly. It's a miracle, a gift that I promise you will be returned somehow, someway. Where do we go from here?"

"Willy, you are not going anywhere if you keep going down the road staring into the rear view mirror. The past is over. The sooner you find a way to shift your thoughts out of your regrets for the past into your joys of today, the sooner you will begin to experience real happiness, no matter your circumstances. Remember what you said? Shift Happens. It can begin right now or it can never happen.

"I want you to consider something and I have an assignment for you. The thought is to consider that deep inside of you is a big black cauldron cooking up all of your prevailing thoughts. The essence from the cauldron pushes through your pores and is clearly visible. So, all these horrible feelings you have been having about yourself are all over you. Your friends can see and feel them. You want to think you have been deserted by them. Willy, they have their own lives. They may not want to be with their old friend dying before their eyes. Give them a break, in your mind. Love them for who they are, and keep your thoughts about them there. OK? If it is true that there is such a cauldron, what would you want to be stewing in there and bursting through your pores, Willy?"

"Love and Light"

"That's a beautiful image Willy. See how quickly that came to you? That's your essence, Willy. That's who you are, no matter what else you may be thinking right now. You are Love and Light. What will you do right now to embody love and light?"

"I-I-don't know" he admitted.

"Write those words down too, Willy. Keep those words wherever you will see them. See the words, think the words, feel the love and light, and act them out. Embody them; let them fill your soul. Think you can do that?"

"That I can do, Julie"

"Start with loving yourself, Willy. All these things you feel ashamed of? Can you look at them another way? Shift your thinking? Imagine that you could go back in time and find yourself as a young boy, feeling alone and confused about his life for the first time. What would you say to him? How would you try to help him see whatever it was that happened in a different way? Can you find love for that boy, Willy? Can you find some love for yourself right now? If you can, then there's a good chance other people will too.

"You can do a lot of things, Willy. Your assignment is this. Go see Marcie. Tell her as much of everything you have told me today that you can. Get it out. When Johnny and Billy return to town, you must go speak with them as well, but that's not important today. Willy, the more you think about anything, the more power you give it. You have been dwelling on some very negative things for quite awhile. They have taken over your life. So, the way you decrease the power those thoughts have over you is to first talk openly about them, and then replace them with more constructive thinking. The more you share what's been happening within you lately, the less impact it will have on you. I need to caution you on some important aspects of your experience. Most people do not understand depression. They just don't get how it manifests itself. They think it's just sadness or laziness. Depression is an evil monster. It lurks in all the dark places within us. It kills people, as you well know. There are as many different reasons why that is true as there are those who must deal with it, which is a much larger percentage of the population than you can imagine. Depression is a liar. It will tell you things that just aren't true. But you will hear them in your own mind and have a tendency to believe it. Be on guard, Willy. But don't expect any sympathy or understanding from your family or friends. As time goes on and you do everything you can to take care of yourself, the depression will get smaller and stop shadowing over your life. Also, please don't expect too much from yourself now. Depression affects your ability to think as you normally would. You're in such a state, excruciating anguish, you just want out of it, right then. That's probably what happened the other night. You will not be thinking much about consequences, and you sure won't be especially creative. Not at first, anyway. It will get much better in time. So tell your daughter. I suspect that is going to be very difficult for you because of how you imagine you want her to see you as that Mr. Success guy. He's not real, Willy. You are. So is Marcie. She is not a little girl anymore. She can handle this, especially if you can. The real success will be accepting yourself for who you are. She will love you all the more for it. It will help her everyday to know that she needs to be herself. It will also help Marcie when some terrible crisis comes up in her life.

"But here's the deal. I will see you tomorrow and every day for the next week or so-if you carry out your assignment.

I will give you one every time we meet. If you don't follow through, do not come back and give me some bullshit that you did or are going to get around to it. This is your life, Willy, it is happening now. The more you do, the further you will get away from this. Do we have an agreement?"

"Yes Julie, we have a deal. Thank you."

"Remember what the voice said. You already have everything you need. We can begin to figure out just what those things are. See you tomorrow, Willy."

8

Late that afternoon, Willy drove over to Marcie's house. He didn't call her first to see if she was going to be home. He hoped she wasn't; then he wouldn't be able to reveal to her the truth of his recent misery. But, seeing her car out front, he parked and quickly got out of the car before he lost his nerve. Walking to her front door, he hoped she had company and this would give him a valid reason to explain to Julie Bright the following day as to why he wasn't able to discuss this with his daughter. Revealing all this was going to be excruciating for him. He quietly knocked on the door, hoping she wouldn't hear it and then he would be able to slip away in to the late afternoon shadows.

"Dad! Am I glad to see you!" Marcie embraced him with a huge hug. "This is the best surprise. Come on in. You want something to drink?"

"Hi honey. I wanted to drop by and see you. I hope I'm not interrupting anything."

"Please come in, Dad. Would you like some water, or maybe some juice? "

"Juice sounds really good. Thanks."

"Have a seat. I'll be right back."

While Marcie was in the kitchen, Willy glanced around her comfortable living room; the pale yellow walls, bamboo curtains, some colorful prints framed and hanging on her walls blended nicely together. He always admired her house keeping, how orderly she lived her life.

Marcie returned with a glass with apple juice. She had obviously changed clothes after work, because she had on blue jeans and a Carolina Gamecocks tee shirt. As she crossed the room, Willy easily saw how much she resembled her mother. They had the same wide brown eyes and smile. Like her mother, Marcie's hair color seemed to change slightly from month to month. Currently, Marcie's hair was more blonde than brown, and almost to her shoulders. She was nearly as tall as Willy, and she gestured constantly with her hands when she spoke.

"You really have your mothers smile, Marcie. It's so beautiful. Did you have a good day at work?"

"Oh, you know, new day, same stuff. It was good. How about you? I'm glad you're here," she repeated.

"Thanks for the food, Marcie. That was so sweet of you. I owe you an explanation. I –I have to tell you what has been going on, so maybe you can understand a little bit about me.

Marcie sat near him on the sofa, turning towards him while he spoke. Willy described his life of the last several years. He told Marcie most of what has happened to him, leaving out the suicide attempt. He also left out telling her about 'the voice.' That was a little too out there. She was very interested in what Dr. Mike McDonald had said to him about the likelihood being that the tremendous anxiety that had progressively built up within Willy had probably brought about depression, and had given him some medications that might be helpful. He concluded with a summary of his meeting with Julie Bright. Willy noticed in the telling that he was feeling better and more at ease, as if keeping these truths inside were a poison that was leaving his system.

"Wow, Dad. Whew. It's like this gloom settled over you when Mom moved out. There used to be such a smile about you, so much light in your eyes. We knew the divorce really hurt you, I guess much worse than we could have known. Now, we sometimes see that light, but more and more it's like you are looking way off in the distance, searching for something, and you seem so sad a lot of the time."

"I know Marcie. I was so lost about what was happening with me. I didn't understand where it was going. I wasn't aware of how I was responding to it. I don't like to dwell on myself and figured that whatever it was would work its way out. Being a father, you want your children to not have to worry about anything and just be able to enjoy their lives without worrying about their sad dad. So, I hoped I was doing a good job of hiding it."

"Well, then your acting career is officially over. Johnny, Billy and I talked about it all the time. We didn't know what to do. The way we saw it was that we had that wonderful house on the island. Life was good and then something changed. So we got that something terrible happened financially and you lost lots of money. But that's just money,

Dad-you still have us. You get that, don't you? You had so many friends and now you think you are all alone."

Marcie moved over and snuggled next to him on the sofa. He put his arm around her and her head settled familiarly on his shoulder. "We love you, Daddy. I am so glad you have told me this and that you are taking care of yourself." They sat quietly for a while. Willy was relieved that the truth was out. Marcie was happy to have her father holding her.

"I'm sorry I didn't talk to you about this sooner, Marcie."

"Well you're here now and you just did. Are you hungry? I was cooking some spaghetti and there is plenty."

"Oh no, Marcie. I'm fine, really."

"That's what you said two days ago. You need to eat. The whole time you were just talking to me your stomach was making very peculiar sounds. I thought I heard a tiny voice screaming 'Feed me, feed me, he won't; please feed me.' Why don't you just sit there and it will be ready in a few minutes. OK?"

"You sound like your mother."

As Marcie prepared their meal, Willy was trying to recall the last time he had eaten more than once in a day. 'Two meals in the same day! What a concept!' He relaxed very contentedly on the sofa as he waited. He began to hear the strange noises his stomach was making.

Marcie's spaghetti was fabulous. As they ate, Willy asked how her work was going. Marcie had an administrative job with a defense electronics company.

"Good, I guess. They just assigned another new employee to me for training. Of course, they are not paying me any more money and I have to do my work and half of his. You'd like him Dad. His name is Josh, he just graduated from college and he asks a lot of questions."

"Asking questions is how we get along. Good for you Marcie. Your boss seems to have a lot of confidence in you. You ever going to be able to tell me exactly what you all do there?"

"If I did, I'd have to run you over with the car or something. It's all classified, that's why I had to get those security clearances. I really cannot tell you anything about what I do or what the company does. Hey Dad, do you remember that conference you took me to up in Charlotte when I was a freshman in high school?"

"Uh-sure," replied Willy nervously, knowing where this was headed.

"I have never forgotten any of it. Your company called it "Game Plan for Greatness" and they had asked you to be one of the first speakers. Do you remember that?"

"Well yeah. I thought they invited me because I needed a game plan."

"Funny, Dad. You were the first speaker. You said something that still helps me today. Do you know what that is?"

"No idea."

"You spoke for a while and then you drew a picture of a big wheel with at least six spokes. You said that each spoke represented one of the significant elements of everyone's lives, and that everyone should draw a picture in front of them of that wheel. Then they should name for themselves what those were. You said for you that they were your family, your friends, your community, your work, your personal finances and your personal interests. So you wrote them on each spoke. Then you came to the hard part. You asked the room to think about how much of their energy —not their time-their energy, was being spent over the course of a week in each of those areas, either working or preparing to do their best work. You made an energy representation mark on each spoke and then drew a line from one dot to the next. If what resulted was more or less round and resembled a wheel, that indicated their life had some balance; if not, they probably weren't going to have a successful life. And if you didn't have a successful life, ultimately, what was the point of working so hard? You went on to say that work was a part of the energy cycle and that each spoke needed to support the others. If it didn't, ultimately your work was not going to be successful. Now do you remember?"

"Did I say that?" meekly responded Willy, embarrassed and proud of himself.

"The buzz going around the room while everyone was drawing their wheels was amazing, Dad. I was so proud of you. Remember all the applause at the end when you closed by saying that everything that's ever happened to you in your past has prepared you for what's next? Then you went back to your wheel drawing and asked everyone to imagine that first they tighten up the wheel so that their energy was in alignment, and then as they got better at this, the energy would just keep going up and up-and then you drew these new points beyond the original lines to make it look like the sun. That they could accomplish anything they put their heart and soul into. Then you added that no one can think their way to success. It was all about the actions you took, and that having the right energy produced the right results. Each result might be different for each person in the room. That was a great moment. Everyone on their feet, excited. It was you, Dad, who made that happen. The mangers of your company knew you were special and they put you right out in front of that room. You still are, Dad. I think you have forgotten that every part of your past has prepared you, Dad, for what is next. You are special. You seem to be the only one right now who doesn't know this."

"Wow, Marcie. You've got me inspired. Tony Robbins better look out! Yes, I do remember all of that. I'm glad you do and that it has been helpful. We are who we are Marcie. I am so proud of you and who you are. You really had my back this week. That means more to me than you can imagine."

"Look Dad. What do you always tell us? It's to just do our best, to be the best version of ourselves possible? That life works out best for those who do the best with the way life works out. So, I should tell you that when I was looking at your bills, I decided the one thing you needed was your cellphone-so I paid the bill. I also paid the past due on the electric bill. You have given me so much money, I figured it was time for a bit of payback, you know. Now you can call me anytime you want."

Willy was totally stunned by this and his eyes began to tear. "Thank you Marcie," was all he could say as he hugged his daughter.

'I know a better way you can thank me."

"What would that be, Marcie?"

"You know what we haven't done in a long time, Dad?"

"Well-a lot of things, I guess."

"I'll give you a hint," Marcie said as she rose from the sofa and walked over to nearby table. Her back was to Willy. Music suddenly filled the room.

Smiling, she started dancing her way back to Willy.

"You know this song, Dad? It's called 'Happy,' this is Pharrell Williams singing. Up, Dad!"

Willy needed no encouragement. He was on his feet and dancing with his daughter to that song and then the Rolling Stones, Cream and other favorite bands of Willy's they had listened to regularly over the years. They rocked all over the room until many songs later when Willy was truly about to collapse, which he did into the nearest chair. But he couldn't have had a bigger smile on his face, especially when Marcie slid onto his lap, embracing him.

"Dad, you've made me so happy tonight," she whispered in his ear as the song 'White Room' was ending.

Willy returned home, exhausted from the day. He had too much whirling around in his brain. He left the car outside, not quite ready to go back into the garage.

He stopped in his office for a moment to check for any new messages on the computer. As he sat down, he heard the voice again.

"Don't be afraid, Willy. Keep your mind on your work and everything will be OK. Just don't be afraid."

"Alright" Willy said, looking around the room. "Is this 'Field of Dreams Part II,' or some candid camera deal?"

Hearing nothing further and ready to accept anything, he decided the voice may be kind of extremely weird, but the messages were good. He had nothing else going on to guide him, so there was nothing to lose by taking 'the voice' semi-seriously. He found an unused black and white composition book in a desk drawer and decided to use it for a journal on all that he was experiencing. He wrote down a list of the messages he had heard so far, as well as his assignments and recollections from his session with Julie Bright.

'You already have everything you need"

"Keep your mind on your work and everything will be OK. Just don't be afraid."

"The past has prepared you for the future."

"Everything you have done has prepared you for what is next."

"Shift happens"

"What lights me up?"

He had no idea what this all meant and what kind of action he could take. He was feeling overwhelmingly sleepy, so he turned off the lights, went to his room, took the sleeping pill , got in bed and the next thing he knew, it was late the following morning.

9

Willy sat at his desk after finally awakening. He was grateful to be drinking a cup of fresh coffee, and for the banana that was his breakfast.

He read again his notes from the night before. He had slept very soundly and felt more refreshed and alert than he had recently become accustomed to.

"All right, let me see what I have here. I already have everything I need. Don't be afraid. Keep your mind on your work and everything will be OK. What lights me up?"

Willy stared at the words. "How do I have anything I need? I have nothing. What the heck is my work?"

He did have the email confirming that an appointment had been set up for the following week with Ed Shields. But the thought of it began to give him a headache. 'Yet another sales presentation. I do not want to go make yet another sales presentation. My work can't be as yet another salesman.'

But then he recalled listening to Bob Dylan in his car the night before. He remembered his strong, immediate reaction when Dylan sang the line 'When you ain't got nothing, you've got nothing to lose.' He thought about John Lennon's song 'Starting Over.' That was just what he needed to do! It was time to realize that he was, in fact, starting his life all over again. He had nothing to lose. What he had was the very unique opportunity to put his energy into anything he chose to. What was the worst thing that could happen?

Willy felt momentarily inspired. He did have something beyond the appointment. Willy had, at least, an idea of what he was doing. He just had no idea how to begin. But then he groaned when the reality of just how difficult it would be to actually start over; it sounded like an awful lot of work. He slumped further into his chair.

"What lights me up? Not a damn thing, except Marcie and the boys. I can't let them down, not again."

And then a brainstorm hit. There was something he had. He was sitting on it. He had his furniture! Maybe he could sell it! He was going to be staying at Buddy's and wouldn't need it. He could put most of the furniture on Craig's List and have a yard sale, hopefully selling most it. Some cash in hand would be a whole lot better than the $8 burning a hole in his pocket.

For the first time in seemingly forever, Willy felt a pure sense of exhilaration. Luckily, he did have some very good furniture. He went on the Craig's List website after wandering around the house, taking photos of the best stuff, and fifteen minutes later, he had posted everything for sale. "Thank you Marcie paying the cellphone bill," he shouted.

He went to the garage for some card board boxes he could tear up and use for Yard Sale signs. He looked around him, thankful in that moment, that the garage had not been his last place on earth. It was very hot though, and he hurried back into the air conditioning.

He had a plan. The best one he could have under the circumstances. He did have something he needed. He began to wonder if there may not be something else he wasn't thinking of.

He would have to think about that when he returned. It was time to leave to see Julie Bright.

10

"How did everything go last night, Willy?" Julie asked as she was settling into her session room chair.

"Talking with Marcie about all of this was really difficult until I started speaking, Julie. Then it got easier and easier."

"How did you feel?"

"I felt lots of relief, a lot of love from her, lots of peace inside me. I slept really well last night after I got back. She made dinner and we talked for quite awhile."

"Good for you, Willy. That was difficult to do but you stepped up and did it. Following through on your commitments may get harder for you as we go along, or it may be easy. But you can be proud of yourself for taking another step forward. And you've eaten several meals. This is good stuff."

"I heard the voice again, Julie. Am I nuts?"

"No Willy, probably no more than most of us. What did it have to say?"

"It said 'Don't be afraid. Put your mind on your work and everything will be OK. Just don't be afraid.'"

"Sounds like good advice to me. What do you think the voice is, Willy? Does it sound familiar?"

"I have no idea if it sounds like anyone in particular. I don't really know what it is. It may be this infinite intelligence that some of my woo-woo friends talk about all the time. It might be God. It may be my sub-conscious. It may be something I am imagining. I have no idea except that it is there and what it has said sounds like good advice. I have written it down in this journal I have to keep your assignments in and take notes as I go along on this new journey. I'm referring to it for now as 'Starting Over.' Maybe that is the first chapter. "

"Keeping a journal is a powerful idea, Willy. It was to be part of your assignment for today, to begin recording everything you can about your steps; to not only be accountable to yourself, but to keep a record you can go back to on a regular basis. Along with that, you should get either a little recorder or note pad for your car. So as you are driving along you don't forget any ideas that come up. "

"I do have a note book in the Honda. I'll be sure it is close at hand."

"Are you still moving to your friend's house?"

"Yes, tomorrow evening."

"Well, then I am sure you have a lot to do at your house to get ready to move. Since you have completed today's assignment already, I am giving you another. I would like you to write a list of everything you regret. Start with all of your regrets about the past, especially highlighting your biggest regrets. Then, same assignment, please make a similar list of everything you know yourself to be afraid of. I especially would like you to note your deepest fears. You have already mentioned several times your fear of being a homeless person wandering the streets. That is obviously a big one. When you come in tomorrow we will take a look at those lists. It will give us a platform to work from going forward. You need to begin getting a sense of acceptance and closure about your past, Willy. Dwelling incessantly on what you think you would like to have done differently is not going to make it happen. You would not have all the blessings that you do have today, like your children, if those events had not occurred exactly as they did. Until you get some closure on the past Willy, we cannot be fully engaged in the future. You can learn from those experiences and maybe make some more informed choices in the future, which is always going to be right now. These are big steps in that direction. Is there anything you would like to bring up while we are here together?"

"Yes, I would like to thank you, Julie. I already feel so much better. I will see you tomorrow then."

11

Several hours after his Craig's list posting the day before, Willy had received a phone call from a woman who was in town to quickly find a home and furnishings for her and her husband. They had been transferred to Charleston and were leaving their other furniture at their home. They needed a furnished house, but had found an un-furnished one they liked better. She had come to Willy's later that afternoon to take a look. Even more perfectly, she loved most of what Willy was offering. She had come to pick it all up earlier that afternoon after Willy returned from that day's session with Julie. Willy was able to deposit $2000 in his bank account. It seemed to him like a miracle had just occurred. He felt remarkably wealthy, at least for the moment. He was able to temper his impulse to stay at his expensive rented home when the reality that he would have almost no furniture hit him. And he was starting over.

He put his suitcases and some boxes filled with the basic items he thought he would need in the Honda and drove to Buddy's house to begin the new chapter in his life.

Willy was feeling more relaxed but fired up than he could remember when he entered the front door of Buddy's home. He placed the two suitcases he was carrying on the floor to more properly give Buddy a massive hug. The guys had been friends for many decades. A white dog with a wagging, long furry tail stood next to Buddy.

"Willy, this is Lilly, our Goldendoodle."

Willy crouched down and rubbed Lilly's soft furry head. "Hello Lilly." Her tail wagged even faster.

Buddy's wife Linda hadn't returned from work yet, so Lilly accompanied the guys on a tour of the comfortable 3-story home, ending up in what had once been an attic but converted into a guest suite. Willy was overwhelmed with joy as he looked at the space he would be staying in. A comfortable bed, dresser and bedside tables, and the other room had bookcases, a couch and chairs before a TV.

'Willy, you and I have been friends forever. You've always been there for me and we are really happy to have you stay with us. You haven't said what exactly brought this about and I am not pressuring you to do so. We can talk any time you want. Your secrets are safe here. Linda is happy too, as long as this is short term. I assured her it would be no longer than for six weeks. I hope you understand that is the way it is. But you live here now, so help yourself to the refrigerator. You can eat with us at night if you want, but I would like you to contribute in some way. We don't want any rent, just your company. OK? "

"Buddy, that is more than OK. It is extremely generous of you and Linda, especially her. I will tell you at some point about what's gone on. For now, I am just really wiped out, so if I seem someplace else, just tell me. I don't want to cause you any problems with Linda. So, thank you. I can't find the words to say what this means right now.

12

Dinner that evening with Buddy and Linda had been wonderful; it was the best evening Willy could remember having for quite a long time. Buddy had story after story to report to Linda about the many adventures he and Willy had been on, many of which had happened up in the mountains of North Carolina. Most were extremely funny, but one was downright scary.

One morning, as they were hiking to Cold Mountain, they had come across a group of mountain guys illegally bear hunting. The hunters were each dressed in various camouflaged clothing and none had shaved in weeks. They had a pack of snarling pit bulls which had immediately surrounded Buddy, Willy and their friend Homer as the three had stepped into a clearing on the trail. It was a very tense moment. The locals had quickly stood, rifles in hands to deal with these guys from Charleston, who were now just standing still, looking about and trying to find a diplomatic way to just run like hell away from these mountain guys. Willy had imagined the theme music from 'Deliverance' as he had stood there, staring at these men. Fortunately, Homer was a quick thinking Broad Street lawyer and said

"Fella's, are we glad to see you. There is black bear up on that hill behind us. Could you send your dogs to chase it away?"The hunters and their dogs took off in that direction without a word .Linda hadn't exactly loved hearing about that, but nonetheless the three of them had laughed and laughed. Willy's stomach actually ached from the combination of the funny stories and the dinner. He hadn't quite finished what he had been served, and yet the terrific dinner of salad, grouper, sweet potatoes, broccoli and carrots had completely filled his shrunken belly.

Willy excused himself early that evening and gone to bed, finally able to relax. Beginning the process of moving out of the other house had released a lot of stress Willy had been holding on to. He was wiped out anyway from all that had happened over the previous couple of days. So, even though he had always been a late night person, he couldn't have stayed awake another moment, despite it being just 9:30PM. He had slept until nearly noon the following day.

Lilly, Buddy's dog, had her face on the sheet next to his when as Willy's eyes slowly opened. Her goldenish tail started wagging as he began speaking to her.

"Good morning Lilly, "he said quietly as he began rubbing her head behind her ears. "Did you notice our names rhyme? Willy and Lilly. Are we related or something?"

The attention was all the dog needed. She leapt onto the bed, rolled over on her back to get her squirming belly rubbed. Willy didn't mind at all. He was glad for this kind of company and missed his dogs very much at that moment. He quickly found a spot she liked a lot, and after a few moments Lilly jumped off the bed and ran out of the room, only to re-enter and roll on her back again on the carpet. This all made Willy very happy. Lilly finally had enough of the good times and headed back out the door. Willy could hear her going down the steps. Linda was down there and he could hear her talking to Lilly.

Willy found a scale in the bathroom, and was still somewhat shocked to see it indicated that he weighed 172 lbs. He was 6 feet tall, approaching 60 years old, and, although he had kept himself in good shape, with his big frame he normally weighed a bit more than 200lbs. He had been eating well the last few days. 'What must his weight have been at last week?' he wondered. He looked closely at himself in the mirror. Willy thought he really looked like crap .His cheek bones were still rather prominent, his eyes looked dull and very tired, his skin was a very unhealthy shade of white. He looked weak, with no definition to his body at all, and his arms were skinny. His hair was very gray, white in some spots. The smile he thought a normal expression for himself wasn't even hinted at.

But he was here, alive, and under the roof of a close and trusted friend. He had a bit of cash to live on, but he had tons of bills, and was far away from the comfortable life he wanted to be living. Worse, he was totally lacking in inspiration as to what his next big step would be. Being here at Buddy's was just shelter from the storm. He was going to have to re-enter it in the very near future. Other than an afternoon session with Julie Bright, he had nothing scheduled for the day, nothing to have gotten up for and not much on the horizon other than the yard sale Saturday morning.

Remembering the image in the mirror and his biceps being so unimpressive at Dr Mikes, he found a reasonably comfortable spot on the floor and did as many stomach crunches and pushups as he could. Willy was not happy with how weak he was, but glad he had done something. He decided he would take a late afternoon walk after returning from his appointment and maybe, it would have begun to cool off a bit outside.

As he stood back up, he remembered the words 'Don't be afraid Put your mind on your work and everything will be OK.' "Easy for you to say," Willy spoke out loud. "How about an idea about what exactly my work is? Why is all this so damned hard? Instead of all the questions, how about a few answers instead? All I have to do is completely change most of my life. How hard can that be?"

He went downstairs to have a brunch of grits and eggs. Willy was beginning to enjoy eating again.

His session with Julie that day had been productive; it was primarily Willy's opportunity to talk about what was actually so good about the experience he was having. He had surprised himself with the number of thoughts he continued to have. When he finally returned to the house, he was eager to take that walk he'd promised himself. Even though it was very hot outside, he wanted the exercise and to become familiar with Buddy and Linda's neighborhood.

It was a relatively new neighborhood. Although most of the houses were no more than ten years old, there were many mature trees, and Willy stayed in the shady side of the street as he ambled along. There were a nice variety of brightly colored Charleston style homes on both sides of the streets; mostly two-story wood frame houses, each with a piazza on one side and well cared for yards.

As he turned a corner, he saw a woman coming towards him with a brown and white dog on a leash. The woman had gray black hair and was wearing a yellow sundress. The dog seemed to have a mind of its own and the lady was just following along, being pulled one way and then another as she clung to the leash. Willy noticed right away that she was good looking and was suddenly hungry for some female companionship. He hadn't thought much about how very lonely he was. One glimpse of this woman was all it took to activate that section of his brain. A part of him said don't even think about it, that this wasn't the time to be even thinking about meeting a new woman. The other part of him said go for it. As he got closer to her, they made eye contact; she looked away and then back at him, looked at the dog and then back at Willy. The dog stopped suddenly and she almost fell over it.

"Who's walking who?" asked Willy, as friendly as he could muster.

"Hello," she replied as she continued down the street, away from him.

'Oh well.'

13

Marcie helped Willy with the yard sale on Saturday morning. He was glad to have her help. Marcie had great people skills and tons of energy, both of which were put to good use. Willy was exhausted and did a lot of sitting, proudly watching Marcie sell a few items that probably would not have otherwise been sold. Mr. and Mrs. Soames happened to come by. Dressed in a blazer and pressed khakis, Mr. Soames was obviously having a casual Saturday in that he was not wearing a necktie with his starched white shirt. It was nice to see them though, and to introduce them to Marcie, who they had heard so much about over the years. But the Soames were just stopping by, not buying anything they said together as if on cue, smiling almost identically as they said goodbye. Most of the people who came by were looking for knick-knacks and there weren't any of those. Although they were able to sell only a few things, Willy and Marcie had fun meeting people throughout the morning. Doing something together for the first time in several years was very special for both of them.

Willy had arranged to donate to Habitat for Humanity the remaining unsold furniture. They would be coming by on Monday. He spent the afternoon boxing his kitchen stuff and his books. He filled his car with all that he could, including his clothing and remaining art work, and then made numerous trips to a nearby storage facility to leave all of it in a locker there.

He left the framed question 'What light's you up?' in the car to take with him to Buddy's, along with a few other items. It seemed the most important question he could ask himself. He didn't have an answer to what filled him with excitement, joy and purpose, but he also knew that if he kept asking, the right answer would eventually arrive. He knew what he didn't want, and was determined to live his life without any distractions. His quest was to find the light in his life again-to find what did or could, light him up.

Willy was completely exhausted when he finally returned to Buddy's. After getting his clothes and other items put away, he looked at the bed and it sure looked inviting. But he had promised himself he would walk every day, and this was as good a time as any to start following through on the commitments he made with himself. His shirt and shorts felt a big soggy from the garage sale, so after drinking some water, he started off onto the street.

It was still very hot and the shady street helped cool things off by at least one degree. Several of the neighbors were out doing some yard work and Willy returned their looks in his direction with a friendly wave, which they returned. He felt was glad to be out in nature, especially with the yard sale completed and behind him. As he neared the corner he turned right, wondering what the next street was like and where it led to. The woman and dog from the previous night were coming his way.

She was dressed in white and was stopped by a bush the dog was exploring. She turned her head in his direction as he got closer. She smiled, tentatively, before lunging after the dog as it exited the bushes and pulled her down the street towards Willy.

"Hello again," said Willy.

"Oh, hello," she quietly replied, stopping near him. The woman looked cautiously at him, which Willy only sort of noticed. What he did see what that she was very good looking.

"You must live near here. I've just moved in up the street. I'm Willy."

"Hello. My name is Nancy. I live just down the street, behind number twenty-nine in the garage apartment."

"What's your dog's name" he asked, watching it doing a circle around her, wrapping the leash around her legs. He also noticed for the second time that the only jewelry she wore was a brown wooden prayer bracelet on her left wrist.

"Her name is Penny, like I'd like to have a penny for every time she makes a mess of some kind in the house. She is incorrigible but I love her."

"Have you lived here long, Nancy?" Willy couldn't help but notice her startling beautiful blue eyes, how much more attractive Nancy was up close.

"I guess so, a few years at least. Are you going to live here a long time?"

"Just for a few months, but its nice here so I might look for a place close by."

"Oh yes, it is. Penny and I like to walk around here. She loves it. Would you like to come by sometime and visit us? I never have company," she asked invitingly.

He liked the idea of a very attractive woman telling him she was lonely and inviting him to visit, but he was puzzled by how out of control the dog seem to be.

"Sure, I would like that. Maybe around dinner tomorrow? We could walk to that new Italian restaurant around the corner?"

"Tomorrow, hmm. Let me think. I only like to do one thing every day and tomorrow is my library day. Doing that and dinner would be too much for me. I usually go to bed pretty early because I get up at 4 or 4:30 in the morning."

"What do you do at 4:30 in the morning?"

"Oh that's my time of day. I read, I write, and then I mediate for an hour. It is my ritual."

"What are you reading?"

"The Tibetan Book of the Dead, right now. I am becoming a Buddhist," she said proudly.

"Cool."

She smiled at that. "The library has a wonderful section on Buddhist theology. You should take a look at it."

"Do you work at the library?"

"Oh no, I just go there once a week to get some books to study and to say hello to my friends who like to sit there out front."

"Well, I'm sure that is exhausting. It was nice to run into you again, Nancy. Maybe I will see you again sometime."

"Oh, please come by. Penny, stop that." Nancy said as the dog pulled her forward again, going after a squirrel. "Goodbye," she said over her shoulder as she lurched after her dog.

'I can sure pick them,' thought Willy as he continued on his exploration. As he walked he remembered other times in his life when he'd met other very attractive women like Nancy, women who just needed to be good looking and he would find a way to overcome any other misgivings he might have had, especially if they seemed lonely and wanted company. He realized he might have just done something important. He had also just walked away from just the type of distraction he did not need right now. He was glad he had turned his back to this temptation, because Willy knew he could resist anything, except temptation.

'But she sure is good looking,' he thought as he continued on to explore this part of town that was new to him.

14

"So why did you become a stockbroker in the first place, Will? I don't think we've ever talked about that."

It was Sunday night after dinner. Willy and Buddy were sitting on the back porch enjoying the last of the sunset.

"I've always said it was by accident. But as I look back, the truth is it was accidently on purpose. This will sound pretty lame. My Dad is a really great guy, my hero in so many ways. But, when I was growing up, he always seemed so very disappointed in either whatever I did or how successful I wasn't. No matter what I did, or how well, it never seemed to be good enough. The only thing that seemed to matter to him was his definition of success. He set a pretty high bar, but since he was very much a self-made success, it was very obvious to him I should be at least as hard working and successful as he had become. So, the very lame part is that I never felt very good about myself and had no real confidence whatsoever. But, I always wanted to prove something to him. Not so much to me, but to him. This is pretty lame, like I said.

"One day long ago, I was curious as to what stockbrokers actually did, so I went to a brokerage office and several of them were nice enough to spend time talking with me about what they did. It seemed like it might be interesting, so I decided to give it a shot. I did get hired. Dad was so proud. I was too. And I seemed fairly good at it and actually liked it for quite awhile. What I especially got turned on by was writing. I have always enjoyed writing, but never had done much of it. I got an idea one day about a particular approach towards investing, and on the spur of the moment wrote an article describing it. Then I wrote some more. And then, a really great idea floated through. How about doing seminars! Getting up in front of crowds of people and sharing some value added ideas with them. Not only did I thoroughly enjoy it, but apparently the people in the audiences did too. I began opening lots of accounts with people who had come to those seminars. I started traveling all over the state getting in front of crowds of people and giving these talks. Then some of the articles started finding their way into some business publications and that lead to more accounts and then invitations for more speaking engagements. So my business got off to a terrific start. Within a few years I was pretty amazed at how much I was enjoying the work, the writing and seminars and totally blown away at how much money I was making."

"I knew you were doing well, Will. That must have been an amazing time in your life."

"It was, Buddy. So many good things began happening. Emilie and I were very happy, and the children were growing up into these incredible people."

"Your dad must have been very proud of you."

"Yeah, he was. But he was disappointed I didn't take several offers to move to New York and be legitimately successful, as he put it. He thought anyone could be successful in South Carolina. New York was the big leagues. He was a fan of Frank Sinatra and took his lyrics to heart."

"He sounds like he was hard to please."

"The truth is I knew he loved me. He just showed it differently. He was doing his best to encourage me. But, it backfired in that I was apparently very sensitive."

"So, you were successful. Did something change?"

"The industry changed completely and I couldn't find a profitable way to adapt. When I started, the industry was based on the brokers being entrepreneurial. I was able to pretty much run my business the way I wanted, with my branch manager's approval. So I continued doing the writing and the seminars, making investment recommendations that made a lot of sense to me. But as the years rolled along, this thing called compliance became the way the industry was being run. Meaning the lawyers began to determine what the brokers could and could not say publicly. Suddenly the seminars I wrote were not permissible. I could use scripts written by people in New York who had never been brokers or actually met and talked with a client. It was nuts. But I couldn't make myself do something I didn't believe in. There were lots of lawsuits going on in the industry then and I got the fact that the lawyers were working hard to protect the firm and didn't know me and what a great guy I am and had nothing to fear. I just couldn't figure out a new way to run my business the way I believed it should have been run in the environment I was in. Then came a stock market crash and then another. My income was all commissions and they disappeared. We had a nice lifestyle and I had to continually sell investments to maintain it. I really believed that since I was working hard, something would change and I would be making a lot of money again. It didn't happen. Even worse, I started blaming the investment industry for all my problems. I felt so much better not being responsible for what was going on. It was such BS that I did that. It was always my challenge to find a different way to do my business and I didn't find it. It was me that stayed in my position. They had a business to run and did it well by their standards. It got more horrible for me by the day. For many months, the hardest thing I did every day was get out of the car and walk into the office. One day I walked in and just quit. I had to. No plan, but I did it."

"Well, at least you had Emilie to talk with at night about this. I'll bet she was great."

"Buddy, here's where the story gets even lamer. I didn't really keep her that informed. She knew about the stock market crashes, everyone did. She knew I was frustrated and pre-occupied with business. But I didn't really tell her that our income had dropped precipitously. What I have come to realize is that I had reached a point in my life where I was really proud of myself. I was successful by most measures. Even though I knew the truth, I didn't want that image to go away from the eyes of the people I loved. I had something I'd always wanted. I was no longer the screw up. So, I tried to keep it to myself. Home became this kind of safe haven. When I arrived the children were really happy to see me, and so was Emilie. She always had this look in her eye of loving me and being proud of me. I lived for that look. When things started going downhill in the business, I really believed it would turn around. But the more it did, the less I talked about anything related to what I did every day. I slowly started to not communicate with her the way we once had."

"How do you think she would have reacted if you had told her much sooner?"

"She would have been alright with it. The money thing wasn't that important to her. Sure, she loved living at the beach. If I had been honest, the two of us might have figured something out. But my ego got in the way. So, after I quit, I went home and told her the whole story. She naturally flipped out. She thought things were tough but otherwise fine. It's my fault. I had quit communicating with her. So it wasn't too long before Emilie moved out. Everything went further down the toilet after that. It seemed like every time I thought I had hit rock bottom, I would crash through that to a whole new low. I started hiding from my friends then because I didn't want to lie to anyone. I figured sooner or later, good things would happen again because I was still trying every day the best I could to hang in there and turn it around."

"For what it is worth Will, nothing you said there was lame. You were trying to get your dad's respect for most of your life. It finally happened. That isn't lame Will. It is probably why most of us do all kinds of things that most of us don't have the nerve to quit. You did. So don't hold that against yourself. You've got more balls than most guys. You wanted to be happy. What's wrong with that in the long run? Could you have guessed that Emilie would react the way she did? Were you guys getting along pretty good before that?"

"I liked to think so. But we went on this white water rafting trip a few months before this. We were going down this river. I was in the back steering. Every time we were coming up on a big boulder, I would steer one way and she steered the other, instead of paddling. We kept running into the damn boulders and ended up going backwards through the rapids. We were not communicating at all and were pissed at each other the whole rest of the trip."

"So your marriage was on the rocks?"

"Hah. Anyway that's the short version of a much longer story."

"Ever wonder what you'd have done with yourself if you hadn't become a stockbroker?"

"Good question, Buddy. I have been doing nothing but beat myself up about the past for a lot of months. Some days, I feel like the ghosts of Christmas Past, present and Future have their schedules off and all arrive at the same moment. But, all due respect, I can't go there anymore, into the past. I'm-we're only here right now. I have got to be looking to the future, which I guess happens every second. I just can't look backwards anymore."

"All right, that's very cool Willy. Thanks for sharing all that. I can see why you are so wiped out. I'm glad you are here and that you told me all that. You are an amazing guy, Willy. Just keep doing what you need to do. Take care of yourself. Well. I'm going to go and find my wife. Hope you sleep well tonight, Will."

"Night Buddy-and thanks for caring. I have needed to talk about all this and get it out of me. It's funny. I've gone from being a guy who never talked about himself to someone who yaks about himself all the time. I kept it all locked up inside for way too long."

"We can talk whenever you want. Maybe you have got me thinking about some things about me that we can talk about too."

"Anytime will be fine, Buddy. Thanks."

15

As Willy sat in the AmSouth reception area the following Tuesday morning to meet with Ed Shields, he was reviewing his notes from their previous meetings.

"Let go of the outcome. Just Pay Attention."

Willy recognized the voice. 'What in the heck is going on here?' he wondered. 'I am going into this major meeting and Mr Field of Dreams decides to pay a visit right now?'

"Let go of the outcome," the voice repeated.

"Mr. Shields can see you know," announced the receptionist.

As Willy walked the short hall way to Ed's office, he reminded himself to relax and stay calm. This was a gigantically important deal for him right now. 'Let go of the outcome?' he wondered.

The meeting went very well. Ed showed Willy the new product AmSouth finally had for sale, as well as mentioning the many businesses who were the prospective buyers for it and the unique benefits this product would provide them. Ed was anxious to get started on the marketing collateral. He was especially interested in Willy's thoughts on how to market the product without increasing AmSouth's investment. After an hour or so of discussion, the meeting was over. Willy would get a proposal to Ed as quickly as possible so the work could get started. They rose to conclude the meeting.

"I like your style, Willy. You listen really well, ask lots of good questions, and then added something very valuable to what we talked about. You did a great job of approaching us and staying in touch by sending us useful and timely ideas. As we talked about, there are quite a few prospects for the new product that we already know about, probably many more a guy like you could find. What I'm getting to is a question. Are you really happy with what you are doing right now with XYZmedia? Would you be at all interested in a similar position here with AmSouth? We can offer you a salary, 401K, health and other benefits. Think you might be interested? We will do this project with XYZ whether you are interested or not, so this isn't a negotiation on that. It is just an offer of a new opportunity for you. AmSouth can really use you. We have sales people, but, confidentially, I'm not at all satisfied with the results I am getting from them. Someone like you could be just the shot in the arm this company needs. "

Willy was completely flabbergasted. It was tempting. A salary? He'd never had one. Benefits? Holy cow! Did he want to keep doing the same kind of work? No way.

"Wow, Ed. I am really flattered by the offer. I would have to consider it, of course. You have a great organization here and lots of opportunities. But I don't know. I will have to think about it and get back to you. First things first, let's get the proposal back to you so these marketing materials and media can be finished as soon as possible. Then we can talk. Does that sound good to you, Ed?"

"Like I said before, I like your style. You are exactly right. Let's get this ball rolling. If you decide to say no to my offer, there will be no hard feelings."

"Great, Ed. We will get the proposal to you as soon as possible."

Willy rose and stuck his hand across Ed's desk to conclude the meeting.

"Thank you again for your most flattering offer, Ed."

Willy was glad the meeting was over. He was thrilled it was apparently going to result in new business and a check for him. He was totally amazed at the job offer from Ed Shields.

But as he sat in the driver's seat of his car, waiting for the air conditioning to kick in and start to cool him down, he also knew something else. There was no way he was going to take Ed up on his offer.

'I really must be nuts,' he thought to himself. 'Turning down a salary, benefits and who knows what else. Hell, I could just go work for him for a few months and then move on. But that isn't going to happen.'

As he drove his Honda to the XYZmedia offices, he couldn't stop thinking about the meeting. He was elated at the respect Ed seemed to have for him, and he would just be ripping the man off if he even considered it further. He could have personally cared less about this new product. It meant nothing to him. At least when he had been a stockbroker, he had believed wholeheartedly in the investments he was recommending to his clients. It was the management philosophical changes that hurt his business more than anything; the complete override the compliance department seemed to have on any marketing initiatives that had finally been enough for him.

Willy needed a new life that was exciting and meaning-ful, one that every party to whatever he was doing benefit-ted, including him .Just the promise of some money wasn't going to be enough for him anymore. He needed to find what lit him up.

Willy parked his car in front of the five story office build-ing where XYZmedia had their office. The white stucco building was featureless, bland and boring to Willy. It was just another office building. He hurried inside to get away from the intense heat. Willy had endured many a summer in the south and had never quite adjusted to how hot it was. But it seemed like it was getting hotter each summer every-where. It was the weather the rest of the year in the south that made living here such a paradise to him.

He got off the elevator on the fourth floor and entered XYZmedia. It was very quiet as usual. He passed the editing room where two guys were busy at work. Going down the hall, he passed another room where the IT staff was busy creating websites. He arrived at Dan Hitchens office and poked his head in. Dan had been producing outstanding videos for many years and was widely regarded as one of the top video production guys in the Southeastern United States. Willy had always found Dan to be a great guy to work with because he was a very good listener, had a good eye for the best images and a very creative mind for integrating various video technology into the final videos. He was terrific to know and Willy always enjoyed his company.

"Hey Dan, what are you up to?"

"Just looking over some footage we shot this morning out in the harbor. How you doin' Willy?" he replied as he rose to shake hands. "So it went well at AmSouth! That's great. You've been after them a long time. Good job."

"Thanks Dan. I'd like to say it's easy if you just keep in touch with people. Who knows? Anyway, a portion of what they want is an animated video that describes this new product. He has a budget for it but wouldn't say how much that was until he received an actual proposal from us. Since the last one we sent him was for $35,000, and he didn't mention that, you should probably assume that is a good ball park number. Let me go over with you my notes from the meeting."

Willy and Dan spoke for the next twenty minutes about the project. Dan added some ideas on top of Willy's.

"OK Willy, I should be able to get this proposal over to Ed in the morning at the latest. I will copy you on it and then you will do what you do best. Go back over there to get his signature and our deposit. What else are you working on now?"

"The usual suspects, plus a tire recycling company that is getting ready to open another facility. Hopefully they agree it is time to do some media work. God's delays are not necessarily God's denials, you know. "

"Willy, can I ask...How are you doing? You look like you've lost some weight."

"I'm OK, but yeah, I was getting a bit chunky. What's new with you Dan, other than working 80 hours a week?"

"Just the same old stuff, Willy."

"Where's Kate today? I didn't see her in with her crew." Kate Adams was a graphic design whiz and had been Dan's partner since they had founded XYZmedia ten years before.

"Thank you for asking. I almost forgot. Katie is down in Savannah meeting with that big architectural firm about that Augmented Reality idea you proposed to them in the spring. They seem to suddenly have some enthusiasm for it. We'll let you know how that turns out. Maybe you want to run that past some of those other firms you've spoken with about it."

"Maybe. Well, time for me to head on, see what other dragons need slaying today."

Willy left shortly afterwards. As he sat in his car letting it cool again, he knew he was not about to go looking for other business, at least not that day. He did not want to spend any more energy that would likely lead him right back to where he had been recently. He liked Dan Hitchens a lot, but Willy felt worn out from simply one meeting with one prospective client and then meeting with Dan. The whole time he had been sitting there in Dan's office, Willy had felt a bit like an impostor. It just didn't feel real to him anymore; there was none of the old excitement about bringing in some new business from a new client. It was time to move on to something new.

'But what?' wondered Willy as he drove out of the parking lot.

~~

Later that day, Willy arrived at Dr. Julie Bright's office. She was wearing a long white cotton dress, and wore a sea blue prayer shawl over her tanned shoulders. After greeting him, she led him to her therapy room. Entering, Willy was glad there was only a corner light on. The rest of the room was bathed in the shadows of late afternoon.

"How is it going with the Effexor?" she asked as they settled into their comfortable seats.

"Good, I guess, Julie. I don't really feel anything, other than being a bit less stressed. How am I supposed to be feeling?"

"Less stressed is good, Willy. You've just been on it for a week and it takes several weeks for it to really start showing up. What have you been doing with yourself?"

Willy described for her his days at Buddy's house, how he'd been sleeping a lot, eating, exercising. But then he told her about the meeting with Ed Shields, and the offer and his reaction to it.

"Well, you're not as nuts as you might be thinking, Willy. It is a tempting offer. That might suggest to you there could be other opportunities out there for you as well. I admire the way you are thinking. You've come a long way since you walked in here last week. You're right-if you are going to have a life were you feel really good about yourself, where you are all lit up, as you put it, you can't keep doing the same things. That voice you've spoken of has an important message for you. Everything you have done up until now has prepared you for what's coming next. You've got everything you need. So, what do you want to do next with your life?"

"You sound like my father, Julie. He used to give me five minutes to figure out how I was going to spend my life."

"Keep your Dad out of this Willy. He sounds like a good man to me in many ways. He loved you. You are just a different person than him that he couldn't relate to. Let's just be thinking about you, what you want, what has excited you, what could excite you. You know what doesn't, so the question is what will?"

"I don't have a clue Julie. No idea."

"Alright, here's your assignment. Make a list of all the things you do not want to do. Whatever job you can think of. Anything. That at least eliminates a lot. A second list of what you like to do. Just the activities. What do you like to read? How do you like to exercise? How do you like to interact with people? What are you interested in? But, at some point soon, you will want to think about meeting your basic needs. Do you really want another episode like last weeks if you can avoid it? Reality sucks. Everybody ultimately has to do what they have to do. You have bought yourself a bit of time by moving to Buddy's house. You will soon have to move on. That's a good thing. We have to agree on that going in to this. You are going to need to be a bit realistic here Willy. Can you make that list? Items like having a roof over your head, eating, paying for your lights and air conditioning, gasoline, those kinds of things. You are in survival mode right now. You might want to look at it that way. Or not. What do you think?"

"I think I am getting a headache."

"Sounds like that hit pretty close to home, Willy. I will see you the day after tomorrow."

16

The night sky was just beginning to turn into morning as Willy began to wake up. He lay quietly, listening to some birds singing outside. He'd slept well and wondered for a moment what he should do that day.

'I need some coffee,' he realized, quickly getting up. He knew exactly where he needed to go to get it.

The 'Percs of Paradise' coffee shop was just a mile or so from Buddy's house and Willy thought that walking there would be a good idea. 'Percs had been his first stop every morning for many years. It had great atmosphere and very good coffee. Since it was on one of the main roads into town, it was also a very popular gathering place in the mornings. Many people stopped in on their way to work. 'Percs had been a regular morning hangout for Willy and several of his friends for many years. But for quite a few months, he had been avoiding going there. He was ashamed to show his face and have to possibly be honest about what had happened in his life. He was afraid of how folks might react to him, what they might ask him. He missed his friends and had felt very hurt that he hadn't heard from any of them for quite some time. But he had also known that what Julie

Bright had suggested to him about loving himself and them was right on. He would have to see them one day, sooner or later. This beautiful lowcountry summer morning was as good a time as any.

Entering, he paused for a moment. The familiarity of the place and the various aromas all felt really good. The colorful signs and wall decorations felt especially welcoming as he got in line and approached the counter.

"We'll I'll be. Willy O'Shea! It is so good to see you," smiled Sandy, one of the longtime 'Percs' baristas. "Have you been in a witness protection program or something? You look great. I'm really glad to see you."

"Hey Sandy, it is great to see you too! How have you been?"

"Life gets better every day. Let me guess. You want an extra large blonde roast with a shot?"

"What a memory! Perfect!"

As Willy waited for the coffee, he looked about the crowded café. Many familiar faces were scattered around the various tables, as were some folks he knew. He spotted two of his better friends, Jimmy Dugan and Ron Healy, sitting together at one of the tables. After he got his coffee, Willy nervously made his way over to them.

"Hey guys, OK if I join you?"

Both Jimmy and Ron rose quickly to greet Willy.

"We've been keeping an extra chair handy in case you ever showed up again .How you doing , Willy Boy?" replied Ron enthusiastically.

Jimmy grabbed a nearby chair and quickly put it up to the table, smiling at Willy. "Great to see you, man. Where have you been hiding yourself?"

"Oh, there's been a lot going on. How are you guys doing?" Willy was elated at seeing these two.

The three talked for an hour, getting somewhat caught up on their lives. Willy asked lots of questions. He didn't want to have to answer any.

Finally, it was time for both Jimmy and Ron to head on to their work.

"Willy, do you want to play some golf next week?" asked Ron.

"Absolutely" replied Willy.

"Call me Monday and we'll make a plan. Or maybe you'll wander back in here before then. It is great to see you Willy. I have missed you."

As he walked back to Buddy's house later that morning , he passed a car with a 'Life is Good!' sticker on its rear windshield. Willy patted the decal. He couldn't have agreed more.

Willy spent most of the afternoon trying to come up with a new idea about what he might do. He thought back to earlier times in his life, searching for an inspirational link. He spent some time making a list of people he greatly admired, considering what they did and how that might connect with him. He went back through all the contact lists on his computer in hopes that an idea might spring from folks he either knew or at least had some knowledge of. But no ideas emerged at all. He pulled out the composition book he used to record the assignments Julie and the voice had given him, as well as the answers to her questions. He read through all of it and again, found no new ideas and then realized he had one to add.

'You will not find your future by staying stuck in the pathways of the past. Find new roads to explore,' he wrote.

"I have got to quit looking at all this old, old stuff and thinking I am suddenly going to see something new,' he said out loud.

He could fell a great deal of anxiety building up inside of him. It started in the back of his head and then quickly spread into his shoulders, down his arms into his fingers, down through his upper body into his stomach and down through his legs. He started to shake as he sat in the chair.

'What is happening to me?' his quivering brain seemed to ask.

Willy took some very deep breaths and momentarily felt better. His eyes landed on the virtually empty of ideas legal pad that sat before him, mocking him in its blankness. The shaking started up again in earnest. He quickly moved to his bed across the room and lay down, breathing deeply in and out as hard as he could. He curled into a fetal-like position and was on the verge of tears.

'Why is this happening? Why am I not getting any ideas? What the hell am I going to do?'

After a few very long moments, he began to relax a bit and sat up. 'A week ago I tried to kill myself. It didn't happen. I am here now. What I have is an idea shortage, that is all. Can I really expect some huge idea to emerge just because it would be mighty convenient for it to show right now? Why don't I try something different? What might be a better way for me to be looking at this? I am just doing what I have always done and look where it got me.'

He got up and re-opened the composition book and made another addition to it.

'You must go to new places to find new ideas. They will not just walk through your door to find you.'

He knew just what new place he needed to go to right then. He was going to the beach.

He changed into his bathing suit, changed shirts and off he went to Sullivan's Island. He parked at Station 18 and was soon on the shaded path leading to the beach. He felt very thirsty all of a sudden, and sat down on a bench to open his water bottle and chill out. Over the distant dunes he could see kites flying and imagined the children that might be holding their strings. He could imagine their excitement, the smiles of joy as they raced around pulling their kites with them, perhaps squealing in joy.

'Wouldn't that be great, to be able to experience great happiness and contentment just by running around the beach with something as simple as a kite? Why do I want to think that everything in my life has to be so complicated and difficult?' he gloomily asked himself.

He rose and continued down the beach path. A family was coming towards him. A sunburned man wearing a red bathing suit and flip plops was pushing a cart before him that had some beach chairs, a cooler and umbrella. Behind him a little blonde haired girl covered in sand skipped along while dragging a beach towel behind her. She was followed by two little boys, each just wearing matching blue bathing suits and laughing about something. And then there was a brown haired woman with the same smile as the little boys behind all of them, trying to keep up as she was carrying several baskets and assorted towels and clothing while a small brown dog pulled on the leash attached to her arm.

Willy let them pass, saying hello to each of them and then continued on. He felt better, glad to be out in the land of the living; being around people, especially around happy people.

As he emerged through the dunes onto the beach, Willy felt a huge weight lift from his shoulders and fly off with the terns soaring above him. He stood for a moment, mesmerized by the sea sparkling before him, the feel of the wind blowing past him. Willy's thoughts were only of the richness of the deep blue sky and drifting clouds, the sight of groups of people dashing into the ocean before him or gathered together enjoying the sun. All of these added together into a sense of liberation for Willy. He hadn't been to the beach in many months.

He began walking along the shoreline, feeling the waves washing over his bare feet. Nearby he saw a young blonde haired boy building sand castles. Willy got closer to him and sat down on the towel he had brought with him, watching the kid. As he watched, he began to remember moments from his own childhood. He wondered what a young Willy would have thought of this older man sitting nearby, if he had taken a moment to look at him, knowing somehow that would be him many years later. Would he like what he saw? His mind drifted further back to those far away years, remembering the endless summer days at the beach. He could picture his family gathered together at day's end, he and his brothers also covered in sand, salt and smiles. The meal times with Mom and Dad were special moments; everyone was then so young and loving one another. He missed his parents and his brothers.

Looking back at the boy near him, he imagined what encouraging words he would want said to himself at a certain point if he were that boy. As he kept the corner of his eye on the kid, he could feel words forming in his mind, words he would have wanted to hear and remember from way back then.

'You are loved unconditionally, Willy. You are a unique and a special person. The greatest version of yourself in the future will become quite real and will be very different than anyone could dream of today. That is because there is only one you and the world is better off for it. Whatever happens, you are loved to a degree beyond your wildest imagination. We are always in this together. You will find unexpected challenges and difficulties along the way that may not seem resolvable at the time, but they will be important turning points in your life. Good things will come out of them; they will just look different than you imagine they will. You will find you have many natural talents and gifts you are not aware of now-take full advantage of them and they will take you to whole new opportunities. You are not ever going to be alone on your journey through life. You are loved for who you are and who you aspire to be, and anything else is just a bonus.'

He smiled, watching as the boy finished his work and ran off to get his mother, bringing her back to show off his work. The mother picked the boy up, hugging him, smiling at him as she told him how proud she was of him. Sharing secretly in this little family moment, Willy felt happy. He wished he had just five minutes to go back in time and be with his parents for a moment like that, just five minutes to speak to the child Willy once was and tell him everything Willy wished he had known back then.

He could never have those five minutes, but he could experience them in a different way. He needed to see Marcie as soon as he could, to hug her and tell her how proud he was of her, and just maybe spend a good bit more than five minutes with his daughter. He promised himself that when his two sons returned from their camps, he would spend as much time with Johnny and Billy as he possibly could.

Willy spent the next several hours at the beach. He swam in the ocean and did some body surfing. He took a long walk down the beach and back, and then he dove back into the ocean to cool off. After which he just sat on his towel and just watched the world go by.

"Your work is whatever you are doing right now."

"I'm sorry, what?" asked Willy, turning around and then to either side of him, wondering who had just spoken.

"Your work is whatever you are doing right at that moment. Just do your best work."

'Ok, this is getting weird. First, Mr. Field of Dreams 'voice shows up at the house, then while I am off to have a business meeting. Now it's at the beach. My work is whatever I am doing? I'm just sitting on the beach. This is my work? Is this a Be Here Now kind of thing?'

But as he thought about what each of the messages from whatever the voice was, Willy began to realize that maybe it is as simple as that. Between the assignments Julie Bright had given him, what he had concluded, and what the voice had to say, he was changing the way he looked at his life and his work.

'I need to love myself for just exactly who I am right now and that is enough. I already have everything I need to do my work; to shift my energy to how I do whatever I do, not what; to just focus solely on what I am doing. The past has prepared me for whatever is coming next. My work is to 'Be Here Now' and do the best I can, let go of what I hoped the outcomes would be, notice what happens and learn from that experience. It is just a shift from how I have been approaching everything. I can do this. Shift Happens, it is happening right now.'

Willy sat up a bit straighter and watched the people around him closer than he had been. He noticed postures and smiles, the completely different bathing suits and hats on everyone there. The different expressions on the faces around him, how each person was sitting or laying down or walking a bit differently than everyone else-that each person had their own unique way of expressing themselves, just as he did.

'Have I been way over thinking all of this?' he wondered.

Finally it was time to go. As he was nearing his car, he saw a car with a bumper sticker that read 'No matter where you go, there you are.' What did that mean? This is another 'Be Here Now' thing, right?'

He got in the car to go take a shower and change before going over to Marcie's, hoping to surprise her with a dinner out, somewhere kind of cheap but good.

17

The following afternoon, Willy arrived for his daily meeting with Julie Bright. He began by bringing her up to date on what he had been experiencing, as well as the work he had done on her assignments to him.

"You have been doing some amazing work, Willy. Look at how far away you are from where you were just two weeks ago. You look better, you sound even better. You have totally committed yourself to this work. I am very impressed, to say the least, and that is not intended to just make you feel better; it is a real compliment. I'm wondering if you would be interested in something as a big next step. For many years now, another therapist and I have been facilitating a weekly group therapy. The members are people like you, Willy, folks who have had a very difficult time with various issues, but have risen to the challenges before them. They call themselves 'The Pathfinders.' They each have a major obstacle in their life, a major challenge. Instead of focusing on the obstacle itself, they are finding pathways through it. They are a proactive bunch, working as group to help one another. There are many names for this but it is most often referred to as a master mind group. They hold each other accountable for following through on their intentions. One of their rules is if a member does not do what they said they would do, then that person is out of The Pathfinders. They don't fool around. They are after results. The membership has evolved as quite a few people have either 'graduated' and moved on, or quit on their intentions. What do you think about this, Willy? Would you like to meet 'The Pathfinders?'?"

"Very definitely! Holy cow, Julie! That seems so cool to me right now."

"I apologize for the short notice on this, but they meet here tonight, at 7PM. The gatherings usually last for two hours, or so. You will be asked to get up at the beginning of the group to introduce yourself, describe what has been going on, all of it, and then state what your obstacle is and what your intentions are. You will be expected to give appropriate feedback to the other members, but not necessarily at the first meeting. You will sign a confidentiality agreement as you arrive that says under no conditions will you discuss this group with anyone other than fellow members. Can you do that? You will be hearing some heavy stuff."

"Absolutely!"

"I hoped you would say that. See you tonight!"

18

Willy was nervous as he sat on one of the chairs arranged in a circle in Julie's office that evening. The other chairs were occupied by Julie, her colleague, Dr. Michelle Meyers, and the diverse group of people that were The Pathfinders. There was pretty much the same number of women as men; several of The Pathfinders were older than Willy, but most were younger. Willy was feeling anxious about what he was actually going to say to these people who were all strangers to him, except Julie. He had confidence in her, so he intended to just go for it and give as real a version of himself as he could.

The session began with Julie introducing Willy to the group, which was followed by each member standing one by one to welcome him and to say what their names were. Julie then asked Willy to stand and tell The Pathfinders about himself and why he was there.

"I thought I knew about Depression" Willy began as he introduced himself to The Pathfinders. "And then I got the guided tour. I became swallowed up in a big black hole that I had thought was the lengthening shadow of my sadness that seemed to follow me everywhere. It was as if the bright light within me that inspired me, guided me and gave my life direction had finally sputtered out. Two weeks ago tonight I tried to end my own life. It wasn't that I wanted to hurt myself. I just wanted to evaporate. Obviously, I was not successful. The way I chose to do it should have worked, but it didn't. So there I was, on the other side of what happened and knew that something had saved me. Why I, of all people, was saved, and for what, I honestly can't completely say. It is the question I am committed to finding the answer to.

"With Julie's help, I have been looking at my life pretty closely since then. Most of my adult life, I believe I have been chasing after someone else's dream for me, trying to make their vision of success my own. There have plenty of victories along the way, in that I've made lots of money and was considered to be successful in my life and my business. But no matter what and how big those successes were, I felt a bit less complete as a person. What I really cared about was my family, my wife and my children. Each of them is one of my dreams come true and I wanted to do as much for them as I could. But, several years ago, the bottom completely fell out of my business. I ended up losing everything. I was divorced by a woman I loved completely, my children and I have drifted a bit away from one another, and whatever financial assets I'd accumulated are long gone. Most of all, I lost myself, long ago. I lost the light, the source within me that is excitement, the why I truly got up in the morning, the all encompassing thing that made me a happy person. As good as my days often were in my former career, when I got home in the evening, what I wanted to share with my family was just how glad I was to be there with them. And that's a good thing. But there wasn't anything special about what I had done that day that I thought was especially worth sharing with them. I wanted my children to see a lot of excitement in me so that they would go out in search of that for themselves. I wanted to know them to know that they too would one day find that thing that totally lit them up, that became their passion and added meaning to their lives.

"Instead I chased money, undeserved status and praise. Nothing that was real. I was in the financial services industry. I was fortunate enough to get off to a fast start, and enjoyed great success early on. As the years rolled along, certain dynamics in that industry changed. After a number of years had passed, the industry was very different than the one I had started off in. But I was making every effort to do my business the way I always had, because it had worked, and I liked to believe that if you worked hard enough, good things would happen. And the time came when it seemed that, all of a sudden, no matter what I did, nothing worked at all to generate income or even inspiration. Each time it seemed I was on the brink of some success, it all vanished. And there I was again, with nothing to show for whatever I had worked as hard as I knew how to create.

"I began to blame the industry. I blamed the stock market collapse. It was easy to do because lots of people were in the same boat; it was real and it was devastating. The story I began to tell everyone was that it was the industries fault and they were to blame for what was happening to me. I found it very easy to point the finger of blame in their direction. But, inside, I knew that wasn't true. The more I came to know that, the more I began to stumble. My ego got in the way of me seeking advice on what else I might do. I put more and more energy into blaming the industry. I should have realized that every time I pointed a finger in their direction, there were of course three pointed straight back at me. Inside I knew this. So I continued to stumble on and on with what had worked in the past, and eventually I was crippled. Nothing worked. I clung to my past success, worked as hard as I could in the belief that good things would eventually come from my hard work, that any day I would begin to make lots of money again and life would be fine. It didn't happen.

"The one person I did not completely tell what was happening was my wife, at least for a long time until it was a bit too late. I didn't want her to worry; I wanted her to be happy. Very selfishly, I wanted the home I came home to at night to be this safe haven I could hide out in. I did not tell my wife that I had begun to liquidate assets to maintain our life style because my income had completely collapsed. Finally, of course, she found out all about it. She did not like me very much when she did. I had not been honest with her, and paid an enormous price for it. I continued to try to do things the old way. That chase led me to that night two weeks ago when I was in so much personal pain; I believed my children and the world would be better off without me.

"For whatever reason, I was spared two weeks ago. I am still just egotistical enough to believe there is a reason why that happened. A very strange thing happened the following day. I heard a voice speaking to me. It said "You already have everything you need." Either I was completely nuts at that point, or I actually did hear this. I believe I did, because several unusual things happened almost immediately that seemed to confirm that message. But I did not understand what the voice meant. I didn't have anything that I thought useful. What I knew was what I didn't have. I am missing the light within me, the feeling of being totally inspired, completely excited about what I really can do to make the world my children live in a much better place. I believe that there is something out there somewhere for me to find, something good for me and in turn my children and the world around me. Maybe what I'm searching for is inside me and wanting to be recognized. I don't know what it is or where it is.

"But that is why I am here. One of the many lessons I hope I have begun to learn is that instead of pointing a finger elsewhere, I should have pointed four back at myself. It's always been up to me, and not to anyone else. Things are what they are, and the only one who can ultimately find my path to success is me. But I can't do it alone. I know that now, and wish I had known that back then and done something about it. When Julie told me about you Pathfinders, and then invited me to come here tonight, I was thrilled. Because I also know I cannot do this alone. I already tried that for a very long time. I hope I can join you Pathfinders and be a part of each of your journeys. I am in search of the lost light in my life, and maybe you are too. Maybe together we can find it."

19

Willy sat back down and, for a moment, allowed himself to just relax, looking at the floor. The room was quiet and he looked back up. Each of the people in the circle was looking at him, most with smiles. A red-haired woman dressed in overalls and a black t-shirt had tears rolling down her cheeks as she gazed down at her booted feet. A dark haired man wearing a blue blazer over a white shirt and jeans stood up and turned in Willy's direction.

"Speaking for myself, I just want to thank you Willy for saying what you did. I really felt you, your pain, the horror that night must have been for you. My name is Henry, and I am hoping you will join us on this journey."

Henry sat, and a black haired woman dressed in a long blue dress stood. "I'm Sylvia, Willy. You touched me deeply. Not with your exact words, but it was what I felt under them. I have been to that place, too. So, welcome."

One by one, the other members of The Pathfinders rose, greeting Willy and acknowledging what he had said and welcoming him.

Julie and Michele looked at one another after the last person had spoken, smiled and Julie stood.

"Willy, it seems you've made some new friends tonight. Welcome to the Pathfinders! Everyone, I have already told Willy what he already knew, that what is said in this room, stays in this room. It seems that our time is almost up. Does anyone have anything they would like to share? Alright then, let's end now. See you all next week!"

Willy stood as the others did and followed their lead in folding up his chair and leaning it against a nearby wall. He turned and standing before him was Henry.

"Great to meet you tonight, Willy. See you next week." And then most of the other members came over to greet him as well. Willy noticed that the woman wearing overalls had started to come over, but discreetly made her way to the door and left.

Julie and Michele were waiting for him at the door. The three talked as they walked together out to the street.

"Nice to meet you, Willy," Michele said. In her black frilly dress and blonde hair, Willy's first impression of her as he had come into the room earlier was that she was Stevie Nicks.

"Julie doesn't often bring her clients here, so when she said she'd invited someone, I guessed it would be someone special. She sure knows how to pick them. You did really well tonight. Welcome to the Pathfinders."

Smiling, she extended her hand to shake. Willy couldn't help noticing Michele had a strong grip.

Julie reached her arms around Willy and hugged him.

"See Willy, shift happens! You were terrific."

"Shift happens?" asked Michele.

"It's a phrase Willy made up the other day to describe what he is working on. I like it."

"I love it!" Michelle responded, looking up at Willy with a searching expression and then a smile. "See y'all."

"Willy, I'll see you for our appointment tomorrow afternoon."

"Great, Julie, thanks again for inviting me to meet The Pathfinders. Hope you have a good evening!"

20

Traffic was light on the Interstate highway as Willy began his drive to meet with Ed Shields at AmSouth to get the proposal signed and deposit collected. As he entered the highway, he pointed the Honda towards the middle lane, as was his custom. But he couldn't help but notice that he was suddenly feeling dizzy and light headed, that his hands were shaking. He promptly slowed down and entered the right lane but continued driving. The dizziness and shaking increased to the point where he pulled the Honda onto the shoulder of the road and stopped, turning off the engine.

'What in the hell is going on now?'

He thought to take a couple of deep breaths and the dizziness subsided. Something very strange had just occurred while he was driving. He took some more deep breaths and felt alright, so he turned the engine back on. AmSouth was just another exit away so he knew he didn't have far to go. He stayed in the right lane. The dizzy feeling returned and seemed to grow as he continued on his way. Very puzzled about what was happening, and a bit freaked out, he drove much slower than any of the other cars until he finally reached the exit.

'What was that all about? Now, is there some new thing to worry about? Am I becoming a total head case, or what?'

He arrived at AmSouth a few minutes later. As he walked to the entrance, he did his best to shift thinking about the very strange moments on the interstate to this appointment.

Willy was curious as to how this meeting would actually go. He had emailed Ed the proposal from XYZmedia for the digital and video project they had discussed, and had received a prompt reply that Ed was eager to get started.

'Wonder what he will say after I tell him I'm turning down his job offer?'

"Good morning Ed. How is your day going?"

"Terrific, Willy. Can we get you some coffee, water, anything?"

"I'm fine Ed, but thanks."

"Please, make yourself comfortable."

As he took his seat, Willy did not hesitate to say what needed to be said.

"Ed, before we get to the digital project, I want to thank you for the job offer. It is a terrific opportunity and I am sure that working with you would be a great experience. But I must say no. I am very happy with my relationship with XYZ and am going to continue doing that. But, Thanks!"

"I do like your style, Willy. We are sorry you won't be joining us now, but the offer is out there for you should you change your mind. I am not looking to hire just anybody, but you would be a real help to us, so there you have it. As I said in confidence, my sales people just aren't even close to achieving the sales targets we had, and I have little hope the year will end with revenues where we planned. This new product is very important to the future of AmSouth. We have a large investment in it and can only make money with it if a lot of companies actually buy it. But, thank you for considering the offer. I have a lot of respect for you starting our meeting with that news.

"So, let's get down to the business at hand. I looked over your proposal. It is very thorough and we are ready to go. I saw that you need a 50% deposit, so I have a check here for you, and I have signed the proposal. What is the next step?"

"Dan Hitchens will give you a phone call in the morning to make an appointment to come over here. The proposal has a schedule in it that begins after he gets some other information from you. He will also need to scout the facility, meet with some of your team leaders and so on. Dan's partner Kate will also call to schedule a separate meeting. She will have her team get started on the product logo, and meet with you, probably by phone initially, to begin gathering the information they need for the website, and then come out to speak with you. If you need me for any reason, don't hesitate to be in touch. I will also be following up with them and you to be sure all expectations are met. Does that sound like a plan, Ed? "

"Great, Willy. Thanks for staying after me to get this going."

21

Willy was in a great mood after dropping off the proposal and check with Dan at XYZmedia. Driving across the Ashley River Bridge into town he had the radio on, listening to one of his favorite bands, The Pretenders, performing 'Middle of the Road' and he was just rocking out, loving life. Willy never tired of seeing any part of the city, and as he turned onto live-oak tree lined Wentworth Street to meet Jimmy Dugan for lunch at the 'Tattooed Tomato,' he was reminded of how much he loved living in Charleston. He passed brightly colored two story homes, sidewalks with folks walking dogs, jogging, pushing baby strollers, or just ambling along, enjoying life despite the heavy mid-day heat of a southern summer day. Willy was glad to amongst the living. Nearing the restaurant, he began the usually challenging process of finding a place to park in downtown Charleston.

He was beginning to sweat as he hustled though the' Tomato's bright red front doors. The place was crowded as usual, but Jimmy Dugan was easy to spot with his prematurely very white hair and huge smile standing by a table, speaking with a guy with thick red hair that Willy didn't recognize.

"Twice in one week! A new record!" boomed Jimmy, his sea blue eyes twinkling as he greeted Willy. They warmly shook hands.

"Willy, let me introduce you to another good friend, Ben Quigley. Ben and I have been battling it out on the golf course lately, trying to see who can have the most putts in a single round. Ben, this is Willy O'Shea."

"Dugan and O'Shea! You guys need to open an Irish pub "laughed Ben. "Hello Willy, it's a pleasure to finally meet you. Jimmy has mentioned you many times." They shook hands.

"Everything he said is probably a lie," smiled Willy back. Ben was about Willy's age and height and was dressed very casually in a sky blue short sleeved fishing shirt, shorts and sneakers.

"Let's all get together for some golf or adult beverages some time. See you guys!" waved Ben as he headed off to another table.

"Great guy, Ben," said Jimmy as they sat. "Couple years ago, that guy was flat on his butt. Willy. He had nearly lost it all. Whatever he has done since has sure worked for him. He's one of the happiest guys I know. How are you doing, Willy? Is your day going well?"

"Jimmy, today's been perfect so far. How's the real estate market treating you?"

"As always, I'm on the razors edge. One side is world domination, the other total oblivion. It sure gets my attention though. Do you know that in the last couple of days, three new hotel deals have been announced for downtown?

Three more! How many luxury hotels do we need! It is amazing how many people want to invest in our great city. Are you still working with that media company?"

"Yeah, for now anyway. I'm feeling like I want to do something new. You ever feel like that, Jimmy?"

'Sure, then I remember what Jerry Garcia said when he was asked what is what was like to be in the Grateful Dead for twenty-five years. He said it was boring. He asked the reporter if he could imagine what it was like to play 'Truckin' and all those same old other songs every night for all those years. Hey, I could imagine it! Holy smokes! I'm in Jerry, is what I say, sign me up! But then he OD'd, so what do I know. My wife always says it doesn't matter what your work is, it matters how you live your life. She's the boss, so I'll go along with that."

"I guess so, Jimmy, but still, I want to feel excited. But maybe that's why God invented golf? So, what looks good on the menu today?"

Jimmy and Willy continued to talk and get caught up with each other over lunch. As they were finishing, Ben Quigley stopped by their table to say goodbye on his way out.

"Nice to have finally met the famous Willy O'Shea. I'm sure I will be seeing you again some time."

"I'm glad you have finally met Ben," commented Jimmy a moment later. "I am surprised you two haven't met before. Well, I need to get going. By the way, did I mention that we are having a party Saturday night at the house? Why don't you come? It'll be fun. You will probably see some old friends, maybe make some new ones. Bring a date. What do you say?"

"OK if I come without a date?"

"Sure. People should start arriving by eight. See you then, pal."

22

Willy was even less sure of what to expect when he arrived at The Pathfinders meeting that evening. As he entered, Julie and Michele were in a corner talking, and most of the group was already there, seated, it seemed, where they had been the week before. Willy sat in the chair he guessed was his. A woman with dirty blonde hair down to her shoulders was next to him and immediately turned, smiling, her hand out in greeting.

"I'm Kimberly, Willy. Glad you have joined us. I really liked what you said last week."

"Hi Kimberly, thanks. It is nice to meet you. Have you been coming to these meetings for very long?"

Her smile was even bigger as she replied. It seemed to Willy that Kimberly was in her late 40's and that her teeth had been extra whitened not long before this gathering.

"Ever since my dear husband ditched me last year. These meetings help me get through the whole week. But I am getting him back. If you ever see a little white Mercedes convertible with the license plate that says 'Whaz Hiz'-that's me! Have you met Tom over here yet?" indicating a balding, nervous looking man to her right who was sitting straight up with his legs pressed together.

"Hello Tom," greeted Willy.

Tom had been looking straight ahead, but turned, making an effort to smile as he replied "Hello" and went back to looking straight ahead.

"Hello Willy, it is so nice to see you. I'm Sylvia," announced a dark haired woman approaching him. Willy stood, shaking hands and saying hello, remembering her from the first meeting. Sylvia then took her seat.

The rest of the group had also come in at that point, each looking at Willy and greeting him, everyone but the red haired woman who was again dressed in overalls. She had gone directly to her chair, looking somewhere else.

Michelle Meyers stood to begin the meeting. That evening she was dressed in a long blue dress with an aqua head wrap of some sort

"Hello Pathfinders! It is so good to see each of you. Before we go around the room and you each bring the group up to date on your week, I wanted to remind you that this Friday night is our monthly trance dance. Willy, you may not know about this so would one of you like to describe it to him?"

"Oh Yes! I will!" hollered a woman with very short and spiky gray hair and dressed in a purple tie-dyed outfit. She was on her feet instantly.

"Willy, I'm Catherine but my friend's call me Cat. Probably lots of other things too! We call it 'Dancing through the Darkness.' We usually meet next door at The

Yoga Center. We begin by sitting on cushions on the floor in a circle and Julie or Michele speaks to us for a while about creating an intention for the dance. They also ask us to begin by breathing deeply as we listen. We are to form an image in our minds of us having just made a big happy breakthrough in whatever might be troubling us as we arrived. We keep belly breathing, taking these deep huge breaths. We hold our neighbors hands for a moment to bring the energy of the group within us. And still holding hands, still breathing very intentionally, we stand. We are still doing this heavy breathing. Then we move apart from one another and we slip a blindfold over our eyes, usually a pretty scarf. You don't look the pretty scarf type, so a bandana or whatever. Then the music starts, this very loud African or New Age or whatever music, no words, just this driving rhythm that just gets you moving. And so for the next hour, you just move to the music, doing whatever comes naturally to your body and spirit. The blindfolds take away your sight, and help to open your subconscious. Everyone has a different trip each time. You definitely will go somewhere, deep inside you. It is very groovy. Michele, Julie and her husband and a few other's will be there to be sure nobody collides or goes flying out a window, so it's all safe. But at the end, you won't be the same. I never am, but that's what it's all about. "Dancing through the Darkness." You said you are searching for your lost light Willy. You've come to the right place. Oh, and you can bring a friend or two. We have some other people who used to be Pathfinders who come pretty often."

'Holy smokeronee's!' thought Willy as Catherine took her seat.

"Thank you, Cat! Let's get started. Cat, you're up. What's your biggest Challenge right now?" The Pathfinders got up in turn and each spoke for five or so minutes about what action steps they had been taking. When each person finished speaking, other members in the circle then began asking questions or offering ideas. Willy decided he would talk about his experience driving on the interstate highway. He did not want that new, whatever it was to become a problematic barrier. He was proud of himself for working on a new issue, and not letting it transform into something bigger than it needed to be.

23

Later that same evening, Willy sat alone in his room at Buddy's. He was buzzing with excitement from all the good things that had been happening over the last few weeks. But there was a very empty place in the middle of all the happiness he was feeling. He hadn't communicated with his sons in some time and missed them tremendously.

Johnny and Billy were now both in summer camps for athletes in the mountains of North Carolina. Both boys loved playing various sports, but Johnny's sport of choice was now lacrosse and Billy's was football. Johnny was now going to be a junior in high school, and lacrosse was a sport he had only been playing for the past year and was already hearing from major colleges. He was a natural at it. Billy was going to be a freshman at the same school and had shown a tremendous love and affinity for football. He was at a camp that had many college coaches working with the young athletes. Fortunately, Emilie' parents loved sports too, and had eagerly volunteered to pay for these camps.

As much as Willy loved Marcie, the birth of Johnny had added a whole new dimension to Willy's life. The boy's came a bit later in Willy's life, at a point when he had thought he probably wouldn't have any more children. As Johnny was growing up, Willy had spent many incredible moment s with him before introducing him to sports and taking him everywhere Willy could. The birth of Billy had been just amazing. The boy seemingly burst out of his mother, and he was an extremely active kid from that moment on. Willy, Johnny and Billy really enjoyed playing different sports together in the backyard before dinner and weekend afternoons. As the boys had gotten older, they began attending college football and basketball games together. But night was the special time for Willy. He would sit with the boys in their room, reading or making up stories for them. The three were very close to one another.

But, just as he had begun leaving things out of what he was telling Emilie about what was going wrong in his business and financial world, Willy had also increasingly found it difficult to always be looking his boys in the eye as they spoke together. He had not wanted them to see his feelings and was afraid they would. Then he would have to tell them what was going on. He did not want them to be worried about anything. He especially did not want them to think that if something was going wrong with their father, then maybe that same something was wrong with them too.

So, in the last months he had done everything he could to avoid them seeing him. He had made up excuses as to why he couldn't come to an event they were in. The last night they were in town before leaving for their camps, he had stopped by to see them at their mother's. But was there so briefly that all they would have seen was his smile and heard him say he loved them. Then with a big hug for each of them, Willy was gone.

He thought about them throughout everyday and now, sitting in Buddy's house, he was thinking of them again. Willy decided it was time to begin connecting with them again.

He sent them each a nearly identical email.

The message to Johnny and Billy was that he loved them more than they could possibly imagine. That all he and their Mom ever expected from them was that they do the very best they possibly could at whatever they were doing, and they had always done that. The upcoming year would be the greatest they had ever had, and their Dad, Mom and big sister would be right with them every step of the way. As proud as he was of them, they should be prouder of themselves. Willy acknowledged that he had been not feeling especially well for quite awhile and had not wanted them to worry about him or be distracted from all that they were doing so well. He was doing fine now and felt better than he had in years. He couldn't wait to see them and hear all about their camps.

Willy felt another weight drop from his shoulders when the emails were both sent.

24

The following afternoon on Sullivan's Island, Willy had just made it into his Honda when a massive thunder storm hit and the rains came pouring down. He sat for a few moments, loving the booming sounds all around him, the huge flashes of light on Fort Moultrie just in front of him, the amazingly heavy rain sounds pounding through the roof of the car. In the mirror, he saw lots of people running by, some with towels over their heads hoping to stay dry after spending time swimming at the beach. He had to laugh, and did, and found himself laughing and laughing. He could barely stop. It had been a long time since he last felt this good, to feel pure joy surging through him for no reason at all. It seemed like magic to him.

As he drove slowly down Middle Street, the island's main road, he began to think back on his day, and the laughter began to ebb away as quickly as it had begun. The only thing he'd really accomplished was going for his long walk on the beach while trying to still answer an assignment from Julie Bright.

It was a simple question. 'If he could do one thing he wasn't doing, what would it be? What would light him up at least a little bit?' Willy's immediate answer to that was interviewing people. He had wondered briefly about how he might feel about a position with a newspaper as a reporter, or perhaps some other media. He was excited about the prospect of starting his business life anew, but due to his financial obligations, he couldn't possibly consider it.. The only interviewing experience he had was in sales presentations, and he knew he just did not want to consider himself a salesman, ever again. Other than that, he hadn't come up with much of anything and was a bit discouraged, thinking he was a long way from finding whatever he was searching for. It was bumming him out. He was very tired of feeling sad and frustrated, over trying to make sense of his life up until now. He was beginning to feel worn out by this whole thinking process he had immersed himself in every day. He wanted to be acting on something, anything.

A beam from the lighthouse flashed through his car as he drove, and he wondered if maybe that was the same as in life, that the light came and went. His eyes landed on a yellow sticky on his dashboard that announced 'Shift Happens!' in bold magic marker. 'How do you just shift?' He recognized it as a great question. He was still fuzzy on how it might manifest itself.

The rain was still dumping tons of water. His windshield wipers were going as fast as they could. Willy noticed that the very familiar buildings on either side of the road looked different through the rain. 'My vision has shifted!' He thought back to something Henry had said at the Pathfinders the night before. "You've got to start right where you are. Just look at it differently."

'Alright, so how do I shift into looking at the XYZmedia work differently? How do I shift being Marcie's Dad differently? How do I be a different kind of father to my two sons? Does just asking the questions begin that?'

Driving off the island, he looked across the waterways and extensive marsh towards Charleston. Huge flashes of lightning showed the marsh grasses blowing violently about. His thoughts became absorbed into the booms of thunder and the pounding rain on his roof. The car was being blown about by a fierce wind. The storm was taking him for quite a ride as he continued on, passing over the Ben Sawyer Bridge. Some headlights nearly blinded him and he concentrated more on his driving, and then those lights were gone and, for a moment, there was just the darkness outside of his headlights. He slowed nearly to a stop and pulled over onto the grassy shoulder of the road. He turned off the engine and lights.

Willy was not ready to be back into the bright street lights ahead, not just yet. He had felt a shift within him. Sitting in the darkness with the storm now heading off away from him, he listened and felt the rain mellowing on his roof. Not thinking, just being. He took a very deep breath, and then exhaled it slowly. Doing so again, he relaxed further into his seat, feeling the car moving with the wind, sensing the rain as it landed and ran down the sides of the Honda.

Finally, the moment arrived when he needed to get back in motion. He started the car and eased back on to the roadway. Willy remembered that he hadn't purchased a lottery ticket in over a week. He could definitely use a large and sudden influx of cash right now and the Quik Mart was on his way. When he arrived there, he pulled the Honda into the parking lot and dashed through what was left of the storm.

Conchita was behind the counter as he came in. There were no other customers and her smile got larger and larger as Willy approached her

"My amigo, you've returned!"

"Hey Conchita, how are you doing?"

"Too blessed to be stressed! I be hoping you were gonna be come back in to see me. I miss you, amigo. Look at you! So healthy! So strong! You have color on the skin! So good looking! Last time here, you no look so good. Today you are looking muy muy guapo! You buying lottery tickets tonight?"

"I only buy them from you, Conchita. You are my good luck charm, remember? You told me that so I believe you. Two Powerball tickets please, powered up."

"I like the way you say powered up. You going to remember your friend Conchita when you win?"

"I don't want to make that big boyfriend of yours angry, Conchita."

"Oh, you no worry about him. You looking so good I forget all about him. So you remember me, yes?"

"See you later, Conchita."

25

The Isle of Palms hadn't changed at all since the last time Willy had been out there. As he drove up and down several of the streets, he was flooded with memories from all the years that he, Emilie, Marcie, Johnny and Billy had lived out there; it was where the children had grown up. He made it a point to not drive by their old house as he went to the party at Jimmy Dugan's.

Evidently, it was a big party because he had to drive around just to find a place to park that was reasonably close by. Locking the Honda, he looked at the reflection of himself in the glass. 'Looking good' he thought, as he began walking. 'Well, looking OK.' He was self conscious about his clothes being fairly old. He hadn't been able to buy anything new for several years at least, other than occasionally at Goodwill. 'Not the time to worry about that' he reminded himself as he put a smile he didn't feel on his face as he entered Jimmy's front yard. Willy was nervous; he hadn't been to a party in a long time. He was glad it was here, with old friends from the old neighborhood at the beach.

The front porch had quite a few candles burning on ledges, so he went up the steps and entered the open front door. The entry area had a number of people he didn't know milling about and chatting with one another. He passed by them, smiling as he did.

"Willy O' Shea! How are you?" boomed the voice of Betsy Dugan as she hurried over to hug him. Betsy was a big, tall, brown haired woman. "It has been years! How are Emilie, I'm sorry, how are the boys and Marcie doing? They must be huge by now!"

"Betsy, you look great. It is wonderful to see you. I miss our days out here a lot. How are your girls doing?"

"Joanie is still at Carolina, she will be a senior, if you can believe that. Kerry is going to be a sophomore at Winthrop and is on the varsity basketball team. They are around here somewhere, or at least they were."

"So Kerry's taking up where Mom left off. That's wonderful."

"Jimmy's out back, there's plenty of food, so go have fun. You are looking good Will, getting skinny on us."

The backyard fence seemed to have Christmas lights running all around it. A Tiki bar in one corner of the yard had a line of people in front of it, and a small tent in the opposite corner seemed to be where the food was. A sound system somewhere was playing 'One of These Nights' by the Eagles and a number of people were dancing. Willy made his way into the crowd, not recognizing anyone amongst the small groups of people talking with one another, drink cups in hand. He was a bit hungry and the tent beckoned.

A table laden with mounds of shrimp, salmon, bowls of fruit, pasta, sliced roast beef and baskets of rolls called to him. As he was putting some salmon on his plate, he heard a voice he hadn't heard in years just outside the tent. He finished adding shrimp and some fruit to his plate and went back out into the yard. Standing nearby in animated conversation with several women was Joanie Simmons, a woman he known rather intimately many years before he had met Emilie and had moved to Charleston. Joanie was the only married woman he had ever had an affair with, and he hadn't seen her in decades. Willy had been crazy about her at the time, just completely loved her. Joanie was brilliant, funny, and gorgeous. Their relationship was off and on for several years until Willy had met her husband George, who Willy thought seemed like a pretty good guy. He began feeling guilty about what he and Joanie had been doing and Willy ended the affair shortly after that. Now Joanie was here on the Isle of Palms just a few blocks from his old house. He ate as he tried to discreetly listen to the conversation. As had always been the case, Joanie had the other women in rapt attention as she finished whatever she was saying to lots of laughter.

Ron Healy and a woman came walking up to him just then.

"Willy, my man! How goes it buddy? Have you met my wife, Shelley? This is Willy O"Shea."

"Hello Shelley! Very nice to meet you. That is a beautiful dress," commented Willy.

"Oh, why thank you, Willy O'Shea."

"You doing good tonight, partner?" asked Ron.

"Yeah man, life is good. Perfect night for a party, isn't it?" asked Willy, suddenly feeling inexplicably nervous again and at a loss for words.

"You ever notice how things always go Jimmy Dugan's way? If he and Betsy are having an outdoor party, you can count on good weather," Ron replied.

But Joanie had suddenly appeared, standing just beyond Ron and Shelley, and Willy's eyes had landed on her.

"Hello Willy," said Joanie in voice loud enough to get plenty of attention.

"Joanie!" said Willy, very happy to see her. He quickly introduced her to Ron and Shelley as an old friend he hadn't seen in years.

"Looks like you two have some serious catching up to do," said Ron, winking at Willy. "Come on, Shelley, let's leave these two alone. Golf next week, right Willy?"

Joanie and Willy took a moment to look each other over. Joanie's formerly long brown hair was now cut short and blonde, which Willy knew wasn't even close to her natural color. Otherwise she was unchanged. She was dressed in blue, and had a red drink cup in her hand. Joanie's big smile, wide intelligent eyes still grabbed Willy in places he liked being grabbed.

They hugged for longer than a casual hello, held each other at arm's length, continuing the happiness of seeing each other again after so many years.

"So, what's new?" she finally asked, before she took a quick swallow from her cup.

"Quite a lot, I guess. How long has it been Joanie, nearly thirty years? You look great!"

"So do you, Willy. When I heard your name I almost fell over. Hey, where's your drink?" she suddenly asked.

"Just got here and I headed straight for the food. How do you know Jimmy and Betsy? This is such a nice surprise."

"I don't. I came with my friend Weezie, she's around here somewhere, she does some sort of business with Jimmy and I'm staying with her out on Folly Beach this weekend, so we came over. Let's go get you a drink." Joanie started towards the Tiki bar and Willy walked with her.

"Are you still up in Columbia?"

"Yes, all these years. I keep thinking about leaving but never quite get around to it. I always meant to move down here like you did. Hey, didn't I hear you're married and have lots of kids?"

"I was married. We lived very near here for a long time. My daughter is 26 and the boys are in high school."

"So you're footloose and fancy free? Georgie and I are still separated, did I tell you that? You need to come see me. We sure had some good times, didn't we?" she said, wrapping her arm in his as they got to the bar.

A young, well tanned guy with long and quite blonde hair was tending bar.

"Hi, Mr. O'Shea. How's Bill doing?" the bartender asked.

"Patrick Dennis! How are you doing? I haven't seen you in a long time. Are you still surfing?"

"Every chance I get. I'm in school in Hawaii and home for a while. What can I get you?"

"Joanie, do you need a refill?"

"I always need a refill, you know me. I'll have some more of that Grey Goose and just a splash of tonic."

"Just a club soda for me, Patrick."

"Club soda? You're really drinking club soda?"asked Joanie, as if in shock.

"Tonight I am."

"Please say hey to Bill for me, Mr. O'Shea. And to Johnny. I sure liked babysitting for them."

"I'll do it, Patrick. Take care."

"Club soda!" Joanie continued as they walked away. "Well, bottoms up." They touched cups and she took a good swallow. "You must be glad your kids are growing up and not underfoot anymore. I sure was glad when my daughter finally left and went to college. I never had a moment's peace while she was home. I sure made up for lost time after I dropped her off at Clemson."

"So, you and George are separated?"

"Yes, I guess we'll get divorced some time. It's been five or so years since I moved out. I live in that house in Five Points we had as a rental, remember it?. Hey, do you remember that house you and I used to meet at, that place you lived in? It's right around the corner. I think about you all the time. I'm selling real estate and have a liquor store so I can drink for free, plus some money in a couple of other businesses, none of that stock market stuff you used to do. You still selling stocks and bonds?"

"No, not for awhile now."

"I never saw the point of that. If you ask me, real estate is the way to go. They aren't making any more of it. That's what I'm into and I'm really good at what I do. I was telling George just the other day that if he had listened to me, we'd be really wealthy by now and he could afford to send me lots more money every month. Do you know I caught him sleeping with another woman? Can you imagine the look on his face when I told him I knew about it? It was almost hilarious. So he sends me hush money so I won't take him to court and go after his trust fund. Did I tell you his father was very rich? The jerk had to put it into a trust fund instead of just leaving it to me and Georgie." Joanie took another swallow of her drink."

Willy wasn't sure what there was to say to any of that so he just took a sip of the club soda.

"So you're going to come see me up in Columbia? I can really show you around. The town has really changed. There are lots of good restaurants and new places to go. I have a great new business idea I'm dying to talk to you about. I'm kind of strapped for available cash, so we can use yours. I'll bet you've got a pile socked away. I'm thinking about… oh hey, there's Weezey, come on, you should meet her. I'm surprised you two don't know one another."

"You go ahead Joanie. I'll come find you in a minute."

"Ok, cause I want you to get her address so you can come out to Folly tomorrow morning for Bloody Marys. We have a lot of catching up to do, Willy."

"I'll be right there."

Joanie went off to find her friend and Willy went the opposite direction. He wandered through the crowd to see who he might run into. He was also beginning to sense some anxiety coming on and had begun giving up on figuring out why it happened when it did. He didn't see any familiar faces, other than Jimmy's, who was speaking with another guy Willy didn't recognize, so he went over to say hello.

"Great to see you here, Willy. You having a good time?" asked Jimmy.

"Best party I have been to in a long time, Jimmy," answered Willy truthfully.

"Do you two know each other? Willy O'Shea, this is Jerry Logan."

"Nice to meet you finally, Willy. I see you all the time at Perc's."

"Glad to finally meet you too, Jerry. How goes it?"

"It's all good tonight. Who can beat a great party on the Isle of Palms, especially a Dugan party?"

"You got that right. Jimmy, thanks for the invitation. I have to be moving along."

"Glad you came, Willy. You going to be at the coffee shop on Monday morning? I want to pick up where we left off the other day. It's been great seeing you most mornings again."

"It has been for me too, Jimmy. See you then. Say thanks to Betsy for me, will you?"

'It was nice to get out and go to a party, but Jeez!' thought Willy as he hurried to his car.

Willy drove up the street to the beach, parked and began walking towards the ocean. It was the same beach that he, Emilie and the children went to all the years they had lived on the Isle of Palms.

It was a beautiful night. A gentle breeze from the south drifted around him. He could begin to hear the familiar sounds of the crashing waves: they were soothing to Willy. The sky was relatively clear and there was an abundance of stars. Orion's belt was visible, high in the sky before him. The darkness was especially comforting. He wondered what phase the moon might be in. He once always knew.

As he reached the dune lined entrance to the beach, Willy saw the moon just below some silvery clouds. It was simply the leading edge of the moon, the bit of light only seen just after the new moon, the moon of darkness. It was like a little lopsided grin sitting there above the horizon, greeting him and seeming to be welcoming him back after he had been away from this special place for so long. Its presence captivated him.

As he stood between the dunes, transfixed, Willy began to hope and wonder that this little grin might be a sign that he had reached some sort of turning point; that it symbolized the lost light he had been seeking.

He walked to the edge of the ocean and began walking south. Many memories of times past came back to him as he continued along; the thoughts came rushing in like the tide. There was once a great gully on that part of the beach that filled with water at low tide and was the perfect place for very young kids to wade around in; he recalled lots of special moments with each of his kids from those days. The boys began surfing right there and he had once watched a teenage Marcie walking hand in hand with a high school quarterback along this same beach. It was the place he and Emilie often came when they had some time alone. For many years, Willy's late afternoon runs had begun and ended in that very place. Each grain of sand seemed to hold a memory for him; each moonbeam had once held his dreams.

But other memories started to come to him as well. Willy began feeling very sad about all he had lost. He was glad it was dark so if someone happened along they wouldn't see the tears. And then he realized that he was very lucky to have met Emilie. They had many happy years together, especially with the children. He wouldn't have missed a moment of it, wouldn't trade any of it away, despite the way it had ended. He knew he would never have had any of it if he had continued on with women like Joanie. He was a very lucky man.

26

"Knock knock."

"Hey Buddy, come on in. How are you doing?"

"What are you up to Willy?"

"Just reading some things online. I've been wondering what might be fun to do, like as a part time job or something, so I've been looking at some different company's websites. Right now I'm looking at some of the tour company's downtown, wondering if being a tour guide might be a good thing. It sounds like it's not easy to get started."

"Linda has a friend from her work whose husband does that. It seems like he really likes it. You would be good at it, Will. You sure like history. You should really check that out."

"How was your day?"

"Another long day at work. Linda said you made 'O'Shea's famous Chicken and Jersey Dumplings' for dinner. It must have been pretty good because she almost never raves about someone else's cooking."

"There's some left over in a container in the refrigerator. You should try it Buddy, be good for you. I guarantee it will not be like any chicken and dumplings you've ever had."

"We'll have to see about that. Linda also said she really likes you, and if you need to stay here an extra week or two, it's OK with her. She then let me know that apparently we're all going down to Myskins Saturday night, which sounds like a very cool idea. Do you know who's playing? We haven't been there in a while."

"A Zydeco band, I think. You like Cajun music?"

"Totally! That'll be fun. How's everything with you? You seem like you are feeling better."

"It comes and goes. Earlier today I had a really bad episode. It seems to happen every day. But I get through them."

"So the black pool, as you called it, is still around, huh?"

"Yeah, it calls. But, it's not at all like it was, not as deep, it doesn't quite suck me in like it did."

"How about your boys, Willy? Have you been in touch with them at all? You haven't mentioned them."

"They're still going from camp to camp. Right now Billy is at another football camp up in the mountains. Johnny is at a different lacrosse camp. We've been emailing. Emilie went up to see them. They will be home in a few weeks"

"Why didn't you go?"

"It's gotten a bit complicated. For some reason, I seem to be having a problem driving on highways. I got a major panic attack the other day; it just came out of nowhere. Emilie has been at least a bit cool about that. I finally told her a bit about what's been happening, so she told the boys I wasn't feeling well. I said in my emails to them that I was having some migraine issues. All of this depression stuff is becoming a pain in the ass, Buddy."

"I guess that you see it as a pain the ass is a good thing, Willy. Did you talk to your therapist about the driving thing?"

"Not yet. I will next week."

"Well, you seem like you are in a better place than you were a few weeks ago, Time is on your side. I appreciate you being open with me about this, Willy."

"Buddy, thanks for touching base on this. I don't like talking about it, but need to. I just do not want to be a downer. But, it really helps, especially when I feel like I am losing it again. It is really good to have in the back of my mind that I am not alone with this. Hey, I was just getting ready to watch one of my all time favorite movies. Have you ever seen 'Seabiscuit?'"

"Isn't that about a horse?"

"Of course. Not a talking one, though. Would you like to watch it with me?"

"Isn't there a great line in that film-something like 'You don't throw a whole life away just because it's a little banged up' or something like that?"

"You quoted it exactly. Wow, I'm impressed. So you've seen it?"

'Several times. I would join you but I need to eat something and go to bed. I am wiped. But definitely, another time for sure."

"Try the chicken and dumplings. Best you'll ever have."

"Hope there's enough left for seconds."

"I wouldn't go that far."

"Glad you are eating again, Willy. Catch you later."

27

"Willy! Glad you were able to join us tonight." Julie Bright greeted him as he entered The Yoga Center for the trance dance. "Please put your shoes over there, grab a cushion from the pile and please join our circle. He found a red cushion and placed it on the floor next to Henry, another of the Pathfinders.

But before he sat, a hand grabbed his shoulder and a guy said "I thought I'd be seeing you again soon." Willy turned to see Ben Quigley standing next to him.

"Ben, man! What a surprise! It's great to see you again!"

"You too, brother. Small world, isn't it. You here to dance tonight, Willy? How'd you hear about this?"

"Julie Bright suggested it. Have you been here before, Ben?"

"Many times, and yeah, Julie first told me about it too. Let's catch up after, OK? I need to grab a pillow and get situated."

There were many more people in the circle than Willy had guessed there would be. Some he knew from The Pathfinders, some he recognized from around town but didn't know. A few others were new faces to him, particularly a woman dressed in black with long, thick gray hair. The circle was forming in the entrance area of the yoga studio. Burning in the middle of the group was a cluster of multi-colored candles. The yoga studio beyond was dark. As more folks arrived, those already seated kept moving their cushions to accommodate the growing circle. Ben was seated cross legged across from Willy and Michele Meyers came in and sat on a blue cushion next to him. Julie closed the front door, lowered the lights in the room so that the candles were the only form of illumination, and then she also sat. The quiet chatter and the room dissolved into silence.

"Greetings to each of you," began Michele. "Tonight we are 'Dancing through the Darkness.' For those of you who are new to this, let me share with you what we will be doing. Some folks refer to this trance dance, others ecstatic dance. It can be called many things. It is a powerful way of letting go; about disconnecting from the way you look at your life, your world, your whatever and experience it differently. We do this in a couple of ways. Some of you may have experienced some form of breath work, where we are engaging our spirits with energetic deep rhythmic breathing. You will be taking deep, powerful breaths, deep inside and then your exhale will be slow but purposeful. We will do this over and over. Tonight we are privileged to be led by our very good friend, Ben Quigley, who has been involved with these dances for some time now. As Ben will explain, you were asked to bring a blindfold of some sort, which we use as we dance. As we take away one sense, we engage another. Taking away sight, we are more easily intentionally moving energy out of our heads and into our core areas. Most of you will be dancing ,but Ben and I, and Julie and her husband Steve over there, he's the good looking guy who can't take his eyes off of beautiful Julie, we will be amongst you , wandering about to keep you safe, to be sure we have no collisions or other possible injuries. We will enter the studio in a few moments. Now, Ben will share some thoughts with you before we begin."

"Everyone, I sit in the circle with you as a fellow traveler," began Ben. "Theses dances, this work has made an incredible difference in my life journey, it has helped me to begin to join together all the very disconnected souls that used to be me. It is such a pleasure for me to be with each of you and hope you find what I have, that we are each powerful beyond measure. Let's begin by taking a deep breath. I will slowly count to five, breath in as I count and then hold your breath. Slowly exhale as I count backwards from five to one and then we begin our inhales again Time your breath to the count .I will stop counting at some point, but you should keep breathing as I will share with you some thoughts that have sustained me."

He begins the count and they all start taking deep breaths. After some minutes had passed, and the breathing has gotten deeper and deeper, Ben began to speak.

"I wish I could show you, when you are lonely or in darkness, the astonishing light of your own being.' Hafiz wrote those words long ago and they continue to resonate today. Please continue your breathing. "True happiness comes when realize how much you have to be grateful for. We can change our relationship to our world, our friends, our selves when we freely express and share our gratitude. If you can change the way you look at things, the things you look at change. As we continue to breath, please close your eyes. Form an image of the one thing you are most grateful for. With your eyes still closed, take another deep breath, and then slowly rise to your feet. Open your eyes and let us enter the studio."

The group rose and followed Ben and Michele in to the studio.

"Start to move around the room, spreading out so that each of you has found your own space on the floor. OK, now take another deep breath and now, place your blind-fold, your scarves, bandanas, socks, whatever you brought, and place that in your hands. Now keep breathing and slow-ly close your eyes. The music will begin in a moment. Place your blindfold over your eyes. You will be replacing your outer sight with your inner vision. When the music begins, respond to it and keep moving. It will be loud. Keep breath-ing your deep breaths. If you feel dizzy, sit on the floor and one of us will help you. We will be watching, moving among you and should you be in danger of bumping into some-one else, we will gently move you apart. One more deep breath…"

Willy tightened a blue bandana over his eyes just as very loud music began. He listened for a moment. It seemed to have some sort of Caribbean rhythm and beat. He took in another slow, very deep breath and was even slower in ex-haling it, and then took another breath. His body began to move tentatively, and then, with his breaths, even more free-ly. Very soon, he was no longer listening to the music, he was just feeling it, and became swept along with the rhythm, losing awareness of what his body was doing.

Images began bouncing through Willy's consciousness. He experienced himself wandering through empty streets filled with decrepit shopping carts, stumbling through de-bris. He went through an empty doorway and was in a lush forest, on a trail leading upward. He was climbing, pushing thick bushes out of his way, and then entered a huge dance hall with flashing lights, sweating bodies were thrashing all about him as he went through another doorway and into a dark cold alley with red eyes staring at him from all di-rections. He ran and then was moving very slowly through thick muck that rose to his knees. He began leaping to free himself and landed on top of a huge boulder. He felt a deep growl surge upward and through him and he deftly leapt from the boulder and began slinking forward on all fours as if he were a giant cat beginning a hunt. He entered a swamp .Fog began to swirl about him as he continued forward, tree limbs appeared above him and gave way to a path that led downward. He could see a body of water be-fore him and instinctively headed towards it; his eyes look-ing in all directions, his nose sniffing, his ears perked for any sound. The tail of another large cat swished across his face, and then that tail rose to reveal a large pink vagina oozing a yellow fluid. There was a blast of scented heat and his forelegs rose in the air. Below him was the face of the cat looking up at him, a huge grey mane falling on either side of large black eyes. He mounted the cat, felt the warmth of entering, the pleasure blasting through him. He finished the deed quickly and then was running on two legs down a mountainside, trying to catch an eagle soaring before him. He began rolling, feeling with each revolution that he was becoming encased in something that became increasingly rigid. It was beginning to crush him and then, he was totally released. He flew up into the air, turning and turning until he slowly settled onto a mountaintop and a great green valley filled with giant trees came closer and closer to him as he stood still, feeling all powerful. He breathed deeply and exhaled a huge rose colored cloud.

And then Willy was hearing the music, a different rhythm filling him, a quieter but deeper sound that was much slower. His body began moving in place, gently swaying and the music ended. The room was very quiet and he wondered if he was the only person there.

The quiet voice of Michele Meyers entered his consciousness. "You may slowly remove your blindfolds. The room is still dark. Sit where you are if that feels right for you now. The lights will slowly brighten. When you are ready, please rejoin us in the circle."

Willy remained standing. Slowly loosening his blindfold, he lowered it to around his neck. He looked down. Seated next to him at his feet was the gray haired woman he couldn't help noticing in the original circle. She looked up at Willy and quietly asked "Will you help me get up?" and extended her right hand towards him. He took her hand in his and pulled her slowly to her feet. Her big eyes seemed to be looking at something far away and then deeply into Willy's. She smiled, thanked him and made her way to the circle. Willy carefully followed her, overwhelmed with the images from the dance that kept reappearing as he joined the group. He sat in his original seat on a red cushion and closed his eyes to re-experience himself as a giant cat, moving powerfully through a dense, foggy swamp.

As the other members of the group quietly took their seats around him, Willy slowly opened his eyes. Across from him was Emma, the red-haired lady, now clothed in a long white cotton dress, her eyes wild, her large breasts heaving as she stared into the candles before her. Next to her was Kimberley, who seemed to be tentatively looking around the circle, embarrassed as her eyes met Willy's and she quickly looked away. Henry sat, arching his back.

"How are y'all doing?" asked Michele quietly. She sat to Willy's right, next to Julie and her husband. "Would anyone like to share their experience?"

"It was wild, man!" exclaimed Cat, dressed in another tie dyed dress, now a red one. "Wild, I was a dancing fool, and was naked in Times Square, people looking at me, throwing money at me. But then I was swimming in a canal in Venice, California and all these very uptight people were turning their backs on me and then little lights were flickering under the water so I went to check them out and they were some kind of fish so I followed them into my Mothers living room. Mom sat and stared at the TV like I wasn't there and then I was back here hovering above the floor like I was tripping or something."

"I didn't go anywhere. I just danced and that was nice," reported Kimberley.

"My intention was to stop hating men so much" quietly began Emma."All these guy's I kept picturing, all of them had some sarcastic expression on their faces like I was just a little fool and these big , black Amazonian women started appearing and holding me and then they became guys. And they started disappearing until this one guy was holding a lamp and I was following him down a dark passage and into some lighted place where lots of different kinds of people were just hanging out singing songs that had no words, their mouths opening just to these pulsing sounds, long tongues making like circles or something and they were whistling."

"My feet were moving but I didn't follow them" said Tom, looking relaxed and happy. But then my hands started moving and then my elbows and then I was too. It was fun to spin in circles and just move all over the place."

And then the room was quiet again. Michele finally stood and asked everyone to rise and join hands. As they did so, Michele asked them to look at both of the people seated next to them and to thank them, to acknowledge them somehow for being part of the evening's experience. Willy turned to his left and was stunned as he found himself looking into the deep wide brown eyes of the woman with the long gray hair. He had forgotten her but now wondered if he ever could. They looked into each other's eyes and then hugged, holding each other close for a moment and then letting go, and turned away to honor the person on the other side of them.

Michele ended the dance by saying "Now we extinguish these candles, letting their light burn deep within each of you. Namaste."

28

"So how was it, Willy?" Ben Quigley had come up to him just as Willy was going to say something to the gray haired lady before she left.

"Wow, Ben. What an amazing experience. I went on a journey unlike any in a long time. I'm still part way there. Your introduction was really helpful. So, you've been to a lot of these?"

"Oh yeah, a bunch of them. Each one is different. You are never in the same place when you arrive for these, so anything can happen. You just may end up enjoying the dance, you may go somewhere else. Glad you did."

'So, you're friends with Michele?"

"We've been living together a long time, Willy. She is the best thing that ever happened to me. I've got to be going, but I was wondering if we could have lunch, maybe Monday if that works for you?"

"Well sure, that would be great Ben, sure."

"Here's my card. Could you meet me at my office and we can walk somewhere from there?"

"Great. Thanks. I'm looking forward to it."

"See you around noon Monday then Willy. Have a good one, brother."

Willy looked around the room, and was sorry to see that the gray haired woman was no longer there.

He said good night to Julie and her husband Steve and left.

The woman with gray hair was standing on the porch, near the doorway, evidently waiting for him because she walked right up to him, smiling tentatively.

"Hi, we didn't get much of a chance to introduce ourselves. I'm Liz."

"Hello Liz, I'm Willy. I was actually just looking for you. I'm glad you hung around. Did you enjoy the dance?"

"I had an experience, that's for sure. How about you? Have you been here before?"

"First time for me, but it was pretty amazing."

"I don't quite know how to say this, but I couldn't leave without speaking with you." Liz was clearly feeling embarrassed and shy. "I cheated. I lowered my scarf and watched you dance. You move beautifully."

"You did! Really, that tops every other wow I've had tonight. So you wanted to meet me because I'm such a great dancer? "

"It's silly, I feel like an eighth grader. Honest injun, I never do this but, well…I was hoping we could meet up sometime, maybe? Go for a walk or dance or, well, whatever?"

"I would like to do that too, Liz. How about sooner rather than later? Some friends and I are going down to Myskins tomorrow night. Have you ever been there? I'm told there's a Zydeco band playing. It's pretty loud but we could leave if we want. Or dance?"

"I love that place, sure. Do you want to just meet there or..?"

"Where do you live Liz?"

"Nearby, here, in the Old Village."

"Why don't I come by your place at, say, 7:30?"

"That will be really nice, Willy." Liz stepped forward and gave him a quick kiss on the cheek and quickly left.

'Holy Smokeronees.'

29

As Willy was getting ready to go pick up Liz for their date, he began a serious conversation with himself. It had been quite a while since his last relationship, and it had ended disastrously for him. That was just a few months before his nearly fatal plunge into the black pool. He could not let something like that happen again. But he was also very lonely, despite all of the time he was spending with Buddy and Linda.

His relationships with women had always been tricky for Willy. When they worked he was at his best. When they didn't, he sunk. He knew that he was very guilty of over investing his personal power and well being into his relationships. He guessed it had to do with having grown up as a very insecure person who lacked the self esteem that appeared to come so naturally to his friends. He hid it well, or hoped he did. But it was there, he knew it, and was determined that going forward, he would do it differently.

'Just take it easy tonight,' he told himself. 'Be friendly, get to know her and maybe it will be great. But be yourself. Accept her for who she is, not who you want her to be. If she isn't as interested in you for being you, that's cool. Move on.

There will always be another woman to meet, and one day it will be the right one. But it sure would be nice if this was that day, wouldn't it?' he finished thinking as he arrived at the address Liz had given him. 'Just be friends with her. And do not kiss her!"

It was a little old single story wooden cottage, bathed in the glow of the approaching sunset. An elaborately painted mailbox out front read 'Jasmine Rose Oakes.' There were many lush azaleas and camellias throughout the yard, interspersed with crepe myrtles and an ancient live oak that shaded the house. Several large rose bushes, bursting with yellow blooms, crept up the front of the house. He stepped up to the porch, noting there were many potted plants and herbs. An old swing hung at the opposite end.

He knocked on the screen door, which Liz almost immediately opened. She was dressed in a deep blue dress that went almost to her feet, a red stone hung from a thin silver chain around her neck. Her nearly white gray hair was pulled back into a braid which fell over her shoulder. She wore no makeup, which Willy instantly liked.

"Hey there," she greeted him in her soft voice. "Come on in, Willy." She kissed him quickly on his smiling cheek and then held the door open for him.

"This is nice!" he commented, looking about at the variety of paintings and complimentary colors and shapes in the simply but tastefully furnished room.

"Thanks. This was my mom and dad's first home, long ago."

"Really, did you live here for a long time?" he asked, finding it difficult to keep his eyes from absorbing every inch of her.

"Not that I really remember. I was very young when we moved to the country. But they never sold it, and then I inherited it a few years ago and moved in. I really love it."

"I can see why. You know, that is a beautiful dress Liz, the color really suits you."

"Omigosh Willy, thank you. I found it in my closet the other day and knew I hadn't worn it in forever. So, tonight's the night for its coming back out party. You really like it?"

"Totally! It suits you."

"Our colors seem to match. Would you like to sit down for a few minutes before we go? Would you like a glass of wine or anything? I have some red open, or, well, anything you'd like."

A white and gray cat came into the room and settled on the sofa they were headed towards.

"That's Toby, Willy. He used to belong to my son's girl-friend, but somehow ended here one day and never left. He's my pal. Do you have any pets? Oh, did you want some wine?" There was a glass on the coffee table which had some red wine in it.

"Sure, some red sounds good, thanks Liz" he replied, although he didn't drink much and wasn't sure how it would mix with the Effexor he was taking daily.

She returned a moment later and sat near him.

"So, here we are," Liz said.

"These days it's good to be anywhere, but especially to be here with you, Liz. So, you had a good time last night?"

"Yeah," she said, thoughtfully. "Yeah I did. I almost chickened out at the last minute. I don't go out much these days, and thought of some good reasons to stay home. But I couldn't find Toby and figured since he was out, I should be out too. I liked the music. What did you think of it?"

"It was different; the music seemed to help me move pretty quickly into a pretty wild experience. My dreams last night were different too. So, yeah, I liked it a lot and want to do it again. How about you?"

"Definitely. The other thing, I, well, I just, I don't know how to say this," began Liz, looking at the wine in her glass. "I have never just walked up to a man and said what I did to you, Willy." She placed her wine glass on the table as she looked at him, right into his eyes. "I don't know what you might have been thinking when I said that, but there was like something happened last night. I was really aware of you when I came in and went to sit down. And then, while I was, I guess you call it dancing, I was imagining that I was way off in some place, like a desert, and this wind was blowing hot sand at me and I found this big boulder and went behind it and it was warm and peaceful and I felt safe and was doing a dance there with candles in both of my hands and was moving all over the place in this wild, primeval kind of way. You probably think I am nuts, Willy and I understand if you want to leave right now, but I do want to tell you this. So I was doing this dance and the music I was hearing started slowing down and kept getting quieter and quieter and I was suddenly so tired and I lay down. And the music stopped and it was so peaceful and I felt so safe and then I was aware of this big presence near me that felt so important. I took my blindfold off and I was at your feet. I had noticed you right away when I walked in the room and we don't know each other at all, but Michele keeps telling me that one day I will speak from my heart without any fear and I guess this is that day. You think I'm nuts, right, telling you this?"

'No, not at all Liz. I mean, wow, you told that so well. I had an experience too. I was like a panther moving through this swamp and at some point I encountered this other cat, but female and then I was chasing this eagle and landed on a mountain top. I could tell you pretty much the whole thing but, yeah, we're probably both nuts. Let's drink to being nuts." They raised their glasses and touched them, and then each took a swallow.

"I was worried I was being too forward, Willy."

"Liz, I really was looking for you after, so I guess we are even."

They settled back and looked at each other, both smiling.

"So, want to show me around your place?"

"Where are my manners? I so wanted to tell you about last night- I -well come on. There's not that much to see."

They wandered through the kitchen, down a hallway whose walls were covered in old family photos.

Willy laughed at one with a very young Liz wearing overalls, hanging upside down from a tree limb, two pigtails hanging straight down as she was sticking her tongue out at the photographer. They peeked into the three bedrooms, and then entered a small, book filled room with a wooden desk on which sat a laptop computer. There was a wooden chair at the desk, as well as a very comfortable looking brown leather chair and ottoman.

"This is where I spend my time. I'm a book editor, mostly I do historic fiction but lately lots of fantasy romances, really I work on whatever they send me. So I sit here all day reading lots of not very good books and, once in a while, a really good one. I fix them up and send them back."

"How long have you been doing that Liz?"

"Too long. It is just an easy way to make some money. I don't need lots, so it works out. Hey, come on. Let me show you something else."

She took his hand and led him through a door onto a screened porch. "This is my favorite place."

Willy could see why. Just outside of the screens were trellises covered with jasmine, providing shade and privacy. The porch overlooked the yard, which had a garden, more azaleas, a large pine tree and an old garage. Inside, there were several comfortable looking chairs, a small sofa, lamps, a brilliantly colored carpet, a wooden table, a hammock and a brick grill and chimney. The house walls had several small paintings on them. A ceiling fan quietly spun above them.

"What a porch, Liz! I can see why it's your favorite place."

Liz was still holding Willy's hand. She let it go and turned to ask "Could we sit out here for a while before we leave?"

"I would love to," he quickly replied and he meant it, while wondering if they would be sitting on the sofa or chairs. She settled herself towards the middle of the sofa and he sat near her. Liz lit a candle and placed it before them on a little table.

"You must love living here, Liz. It really is fabulous" he said, looking about him.

"Yes, I do. But like I said, it get's lonely sometimes. That's why Michele said I need to get out. So I did and that's how I met you."

"Or, it's how I met you."

They touched glasses again.

"Jasmine Rose Oakes? That's really beautiful. Why is that on your mailbox?"

Liz laughed. "When I was a little girl, I really hated my name. Eliza Oakes sounded so old; it was my grandmother's name. I loved flowers, I always have and my favorites were roses and jasmine. So, I made up a name for myself. I was Jasmine Rose Oakes. I tried to talk mother into changing my name but she wouldn't hear of it. So, it became my secret name. I didn't mind being called Lizzie, which my brother Tom changed to Dizzy Lizzy. So, I hung on to that name. I had to call my business something so it's called Jasmine Rose Oakes, book editors. Makes it sound like there's a bunch of us, but it's just me. I put it on the mailbox because sometimes I get a different person delivering mail and I didn't want any confusion. Some of the manuscripts come by snail mail. But it's really there because every time I see that name, I feel at home."

"It's really beautiful Liz. But Liz is really nice too. The zee sound keeps going on, you know."

"You can call me whatever you want, Willy."

"We'll see. I like the idea of people naming themselves, don't you?"

"What would you name yourself?"

"Thundering Snow."

"Thundering Snow! That's a great name! Why would you call yourself that?"

"Either I still want to be an Indian one day when I grow up, or it's because when I was a kid, sometimes when it was snowing, I liked to just stand outside and experience the falling snow, especially at night, I liked the way it felt landing on my face, and then melting. I listened to the sound it made coming down. It's a very cool thing to listen to if you can get quiet enough. It is, of course, obviously a very soft, very gentle sound, but it is there if you really listen. I thought for the longest time that I'd like to be able to one day be so quiet inside, the snow would seem to be thundering down, so that is where it comes from."

"That was beautiful Willy, so exquisite. I'd like to get rid of all the chatter going on in my mind. Sometimes it's like when you're out driving on a long trip and you're far from a city and you try to find a radio station to listen to but all these other stations keep jumping in and out. Not sure what I'm listening to. So I love your thundering snow. We should go to the mountains sometime in the winter when it is snowing so we can listen. "

"Lizzzz, listen to your name. Can you hear the long z? A bunch of years ago, when I began trying to meditate, I really struggled with it. For one thing, I have an active body; it just won't be still for very long. I had a very difficult time being quiet inside. I worried that meditating as I knew it was separating me from the world around me. So, I often thought back to those very wonderful moments when I would stand there or sometimes turn in a circle with my eyes closed and feel the snow, listening to it land. So, it became easier for me to just focus on my breathing, to actively listen to whatever sounds were around me, to totally feel whatever I was touching. I wanted to be a part of whatever was going on. Does that make any sense to you, Liz?"

"I've never thought of it that way before. Yeah Willy, yeah just shift the way we're trying to experience things. Listening, really experiencing listening would be a lot easier for me than trying to be completely quiet. Of course, you can't hear anything while you're talking. Does it make you uncomfortable to just be quiet with someone, Willy? If there's two people sitting together and no one is speaking at all for a little while, is that a bad thing?"

"It's a good thing, maybe the best part of a true friendship is when there isn't any just chatter going on. Just really being present with someone, without having to do anything other than to really be in that place and nowhere else. So, being quiet seems like the real deal to me.."

Willy and Liz spent a moment just looking into each other's eyes, each of them feeling something special was happening as they sat together on this sofa, while around them the shadows of late afternoon had dissolved into twilight.

"So, not to pry, but, is Michele a friend?"

"Yes, but she's my therapist too. How do you know her?"

177

"Well, Julie Bright is my therapist. She got me involved with a group therapy she facilitates with Michele. I only recently started that. Michele told me there about the 'Dancing through the Darkness' and it seemed like it might be pretty interesting, or just something new to try. "

"Where do you live, Willy? What do you do? I don't know anything about you, other than that you're a good dancer."

"Easy for you to say. Next time I'll do the peeking. I guess you could say my life is in a highly transitional state right now and I am staying with some good friends, not all that far from here. I'm trying to figure some things out, like what do I want to be when I grow up and the Indians don't seem to be an option."

"Is that why you are seeing Julie?"

"That's only part of it .There's been a lot going on with me lately."

Willy felt some anxiety building. He liked Liz more by the minute, and is not sure what to say about his life. He was beginning to feel the wine a bit and he knew he better be careful because he might start revealing more about himself and his feelings than he would if he were completely sober. But then he remembered he just needed to be himself and she could either like him or not.

"I don't normally talk much about my life, at least until lately, Liz. But you, there's something about talking with you that makes me feel like we are really old friends and well, I know there's a lot I would like to tell you. Maybe not tonight, though. OK? Does that seem kind of weird?"

"Funny you say that. I was just thinking about how familiar this feels, like a déjà vu only I know it's new, sitting here with you, the light flickering, the night sounds starting, you looking so handsome , so assured, so comforting, like I can say anything at all and you get it. So I'm kind of back at you with the does that sound weird question."

Willy reached over and took Liz's hand, and they turned towards one another. Liz placed her other hand on top of Willy's. They looked into each other's eyes again for a long moment, and the small smiles they were sharing grew into larger ones.

"Do you still feel like going down to Myskyns?" Willy asked.

"The truth is whatever you'd like to do is fine with me. But I am really enjoying this quiet time talking. I have some food if you are at all hungry. That includes some dessert. Would you like to eat something? "

"I can resist anything except temptation. I am actually a bit hungry. Maybe we can go to Myskyns another night."

Willy and Liz spent the rest of the evening on the porch, after munching on some shrimp, vegetables and Blueberry pie.

"How did you know that's my all time favorite pie?" he asked.

"I don't reveal all my secrets at once," she replied.

It was that kind of an evening for Liz and Willy.

30

Willy woke late the following morning, stretching luxurious-ly as images of Liz drifted peacefully through his thoughts.

Then he sat up suddenly. 'Oh crap!' he thought. 'I have to tell her about…How do I tell her?'

He sank back on to the bed, rolled on to his side and wanted desperately to just disappear, to not have to own up to the truth about the past months of his life and what a loser she was about to discover him to be. "What did I do to deserve all this? Why can't it just go away? I was so happy last night, and she was too. I didn't even try to kiss her, but I could have. What am I going to do? I'm supposed to have dinner with her tonight." He spent his next few moments sinking into the black pool.

And then he sat back up, swung his legs off the bed and got up. "Screw it. I'll just tell her. It's not totally who I am, just a part of me. It's the truth, part of the truth, but not my entire story. Damn it though."

And then the voice showed up. "Shift Happens."

"Shift happens," repeated Willy. So, what needs to shift here? And the answer was so obvious, he felt like an idiot. "I've been so worried about how everyone else looks at me.

How sick I became of being thought of as a salesman, an insincere person. I didn't level with Emilie about how things really were until it was too late because I wanted her to think I was something I wasn't, even though she said she wouldn't have cared. I've been hiding from my boys. Wouldn't today be a good day to climb out of the black pool for awhile and be real with somebody? If Liz never wants to see me again, that's OK because I will be proud of myself for telling her the truth. I have a lot to be proud of, actually. Look at all I have done. Just because it didn't measure up to someone else's standards of real success doesn't mean that a lot of what I have done doesn't mean a lot to me. I have to shift the way I look at myself, my life, to the way I see it. That's all. Can you do that Willy, like today, right now? Get your ass in gear and go do something fun, like walking downstairs and hanging out with Buddy and Linda and finding out about what you missed at Myskins last night.'

31

Willy sat in the Honda for a moment in front of Liz's house, just looking at the house, the yard, the neighborhood. He was trying to imagine who her parents were, what their lives might have been like. He thought it was a very fine house; it looked like someone's home. Being a little girl here must have been very sweet, he imagined. He picked up the flowers he'd picked from Linda's garden and the package of flounder from the seafood store and headed to the house.

He found a note on the door from Liz, saying he should just come in because she was probably still out in the garden. As he entered the kitchen, he quickly spotted a vase and added some water to it, then the handful of yellow daisies and black-eyed Susan's. He placed the vase on her kitchen table and put the fish into the refrigerator, before walking through the porch into the backyard. The sun was still bright but shadows were beginning to lengthen across the grass.

He didn't see Liz at first. The garden had a profusion of sunflowers, tomatoes, climbing vines, pepper plants, and as he got closer, he could see spinach and lettuce, as well as some purple and orange irises. Liz came walking out of the old garage next to the garden with a basket. She was wearing a wide brimmed straw hat, a white blouse, and blue jeans. The afternoon light suited her well. Her white gray hair fell down over her shoulders. She changed direction as she saw him, and seemed to be swinging her basket back and forth as she strolled towards Willy. Her smile lit up her face.

"I was just thinking about you, and here you are."

"Sweet Jasmine Rose! Sorry I left my camera home, Liz. You could not look anymore extra beautiful than you do right at this moment. How are you doing?"

"Better now," she replied as she continued walking directly to him, her eyes focused on his face, only stopping just before him, her nose touching his.

"Do you know what I have wanted to do all day, Willy?" she whispered.

He didn't have to respond with words. Softly, his lips found hers and they kissed, very gently at first and then a surge of passion raced through Willy and he pulled her closer still. Liz's arms wrapped around his waist and they continued to kiss passionately for a few moments. Gently, he pulled his lips away from hers. Liz's eyes opened, just slightly, to gaze into his.

"Oh brother," was all she could say, and then she laughed. "I'm glad we got that settled. Help me grab a few things, will you."

Taking his hand, they entered the garden and picked some tomatoes, a few cucumbers, a green pepper, romaine lettuce, and then pulled up several carrots, placing all of it into the basket. Willy carried the basket as they strolled back to the house hand in hand.

"For me!"

She noticed the flowers right away as they came into the kitchen.

"You are so sweet, Willy. I really cannot remember the last time anyone has brought me flowers. They are beautiful. Thank you." Her arms wrapped again around his waist, looking up at him.

"Are you my boyfriend?"

"Only if you are my girlfriend."

"You better believe it."

"We don't really know each other Liz. I don't know if we are going too fast, but this seems pretty right to me. Let's just talk about whatever we need to if we think we need to .But, you sure fit perfectly, right where you are."

"I think we're going at just the right speed, Willy. Except, well..." and she stepped away from him, a bit of concern on her face. "Maybe we should talk a little. There is something you should know about me. Let's go sit down."

Willy followed her into the living room, thinking about the little speech he had all planned to tell her about himself. They sat on the sofa.

"Liz, before you say anything, there was something I need to tell you. I think you are fabulous. I really want to know all about you. But you need to know about me. The good, the bad, and the ugly. You see, the reason why Julie is my therapist now, why am seeing her as a therapist is that, well, I, I have had this really bad time in my life. I had become depressed, only I didn't know that's what it was. Life just sucked a big one. So, about a month ago, I had gotten so low, so out of it, so at a complete end, there was so much pain, I, I, well I tried to ...end it all one night. But it didn't happen and so I went to see Julie, and my doctor, and now I am on some medication and I am seeing Julie pretty often and trying to look at my life differently. I didn't plan on meeting you, and then I did and I had such a good time last night. But when I woke up this morning, first I was really happy and then got all upset that maybe I hadn't been honest with you because I really was happy, but knew I needed to tell you about this right now, so if you want to change your mind about being my brand new girlfriend it is OK and maybe you should. It's not like I need someone to take care of me, but I am probably going to want to talk about this and its, well, depressing and I hope I just made a whole lot of sense to you because I think I just went all over the place with what I said."

'Willy, wow! A month ago? Wowzer, I mean, thank you for telling me all that and trusting that it was OK, cause it was, it is, and it will always be alright for you to tell me whatever you need to, because how else are we going to get along and be very good friends with one another if we don't? I never would have guessed, to tell you the truth. You seem so happy, so like you've got both feet on the ground. I know all about depression Willy, and that's what I was going to tell you about me and how Michele came to tell me I need to get out of the house more, and to ask for what I want. I...never in my life have I just walked up to a guy and basically said, hey let's go on a date. But I saw you and couldn't quit looking and then there I was literally at your feet. See, I tried to kill myself once, not like hurt myself, you know, I just wanted to become a sparrow or some other bird and just fly away and never come back, never have to think about anything ever again, just fly all over and not think.. I was so afraid you wouldn't understand and think I am a nutcase, which I probably am anyway, but I was afraid to tell you and then you told me and I think that is, well it's the most romantic thing you could have done Willy, to tell me what you did. And now I've told you. So what do you think about you and me right now?"

"I think I am truly crazy about you, Liz."

They moved towards each other and wrapped their arms around each other, looking happily into each other faces, their eyes connecting, their bodies moving even closer. The energy charged embrace continued to build. Willy kissed Liz, and the kiss grew deeper and deeper. As he held her again, Willy suddenly felt something wet land on his neck and guessed it was a tear. They moved as one to the sofa and held each other for quite a while.

32

Willy looked at Ben's business card again. He knew downtown Charleston pretty well, he thought, especially Ansonborough. It was almost noon and he made it a point to be a bit early for his appointments. He pulled his phone out, opened Google Maps, entered the address and started walking further down Anson St. He found a bricked path he didn't recall ever noticing before, and the phone told him to turn left, that he was 50 feet from his destination, 0 Marley Lane.

At the end of the brick path stood a two story wooden house, painted a pale blue with porches on each floor. A wooden sign read The BenQ Company. As Willy stepped onto the porch landing, the front door of the building opened and Matthew Marshall came walking out.

"I say, it's Willy O'Shea!"

"Matthew! Holy cow, what a surprise! How have you been doing?" Willy hadn't seen his old buddy in some time, but Matthew didn't seem to have changed a bit; still the same tall, thin figure with blonde hair tumbling down below his ears, deep blue eyes and a charismatic smile.

They hugged for a moment.

"What are you up to Matthew? I didn't know you were in town."

"Been back for just a little while. I'm staying out at Whistling Dixie. Why don't you come out sometime, like real soon? We can hangout, play some golf, fish, whatever. It will be just like the old times!"

"Yeah, I will do that. You still have the same cell number and everything?"

"Yeah man. I lose that number and I am cooked, you know. What are you doing here, my friend?"

"I have a meeting with Ben? How about you?"

"Same. We were talking over some things. He's real good to bounce ideas off of."

"Listen, I have got to cut this short. I'll call you soon."

"Yeah man."

Willy went inside. The entry area of Ben's building was all wooden. The floors were wide planks, maybe of oak, the walls some sort of cedar. A young woman with bright blue eyes under very short brown hair sat behind a desk, smiling and asking how she could help. Above her was a John Doyle painting of a marlin dancing across a wave. A potted palm sat in a corner. The place was well lit with natural sunlight streaming through tall windows. A wooden stairway led up, and hallways went right and left. Several comfortable rattan chairs faced an old brown leather sofa across from the desk.

"I'm Willy O'Shea, here to see Ben Quigley."

"Hello Mr O'Shea. I'm Sheila," she said with an engaging smile. "Ben's expecting you. He's down at the end of the hallway to your right."

"Thanks Sheila, nice to meet you."

Willy took a moment going down the hallway as he admired each of the works of art displayed on each wall. Charleston was home to a growing number of world class painters and photographers, and many of them were represented on those walls. There was a large black and white photo of a live oak hanging over a creek he had never seen before.

"Hello Ben, thanks for inviting me."

Ben Quigley was seated behind a large table with a laptop and a number of piles of paper before him. He pushed back his chair to rise and greet Willy. Today he was wearing a buttoned down white shirt and dark gray slacks.

"Thank you for coming down here, Willy. Did you have any trouble finding us?"

"That's why God invented Google Maps, I guess. You have a wonderful office, Ben. Have you been here for very long?"

"Oh sure, quite a while. Please, have a seat. Can I get you anything- water, coffee?"

"I'm fine thanks," Willy replied as he settled into a comfortable chair."It was nice to see Matthew Marshall as I was arriving. Have you known him long?"

"You know Matthew? Matty and I are old pals. We sailed to Bermuda with some guys a while back, that's how we met, and we play golf a good bit. How about you, Willy? Have you been out to his place?"

"Whistling Dixie is one of my favorite places on the planet. I thought you looked familiar the other day. Maybe we have seen each other out there. Charleston's still a small town in a lot of ways. So, what is The Ben Q Company? What do you do here?"

"Ah, I like a guy who get's right to it. Why don't I tell you a little here and the rest over lunch? I thought we'd just pop over to Mama Jo's Café since it's just out the back door, if that's OK with you."

"Sure, great place. She has the best fried pickles I've ever had."

As Ben leaned forward, elbows on the desk, sunlight filtered through his red curly hair, and Willy imagined it glowed, as Ben's eyes seemed to.

"Willy, basically we are business consultants, which means we solve problems for people either before they've happened or after. I've been doing this a long time. Once I was a banker, and then it changed, sort of like when Mae West once said that she used to be Snow White and then she drifted. That's us. We get a lot of referrals from lenders who have a customer they send our way. And there is some word of mouth. We don't really market ourselves very well, but so far so good. But there are plenty of opportunities out there for a little company like ours, which is one of the reasons why I wanted to meet you. Plus, we seem to have a growing number of friends and interests in common. Let's go over to Mama Jo's and we can talk some more about this."

It was indeed a short walk to the best Gullah restaurant in downtown Charleston. On the outside, it was just an old, possibly cinder block building with very faded red paint and only a few dingy windows. It was very definitely not a typically old downtown Charleston kind of place. But the various aromas opened your nose right up as you walked through the door. As they entered, both Willy and Ben said hello to folks they knew either leaving with a most satisfied expression on their faces, or were in line waiting to order, as they were. Willy glanced up at the menu on the white board hanging over the old counter. Most of the meals were hand written in either black or blue magic marker, but each featured chicken, shrimp, crab, or some fish. It was impossible to not order something good at Mama Jo's.

After placing their orders, Ben led the way to a wooden table against one of the walls.

"The good news is Mama's is so close to my place, I get to come here a lot. The only bad news is that the food is always so good, I sometimes forget there are plenty of other great places to eat all around here. How long have you been in Charleston, Willy?"

"Pretty close to twenty-five years now, Ben. I have never lived anywhere this long, so I guess it is home, even though I'm still a Yankee according to a lot of people. My kid's are Southern though, my daughter was born in Columbia before we came here, and my two boys were born here, so I can say I am related to Charlestonians. How about you, do you have any children?"

"A daughter in Colorado and a son up at Chapel Hill, not in school, he just likes living there. He dropped out of college long ago and never left town."

"Yeah, I know some guys like that. Have you been in Charleston for long?"

"All of my life, except for a few years. I was up north, hated the winters and came back. I went to college in Boston and finished at the College. Then I got a job at Broad Street Bank and Trust and did that for twelve years or so, met a lot of good people, learned a bunch about how to lose money and figured if I just didn't do the wrong things maybe I'd find some right ones. It's worked out, mostly pretty well. That's how I first met Jimmy Dugan, he was selling houses back then, sold a bunch and he was in the offices a lot. He had a lot of good things to say about you, Willy, when I asked him. He wouldn't mind me saying this, but he also said you were someone who had been pretty successful, but now it seemed like something happen with you that changed that. Jimmy said he hadn't laid an eye on you in quite a while, hadn't heard from you, and then you showed up one day looking like your insides had blown out of you and you were like a shell of the guy he knew. Don't get me wrong, he's glad you showed up and he likes and respects and cares about you, to say what he did. See, I had something happen too, a few years ago now, so maybe I know a bit about what kinds of things can happen to good guys and gals. Life can really suck some times, and then it can also get real better again, right quick. That OK with you that Jimmy said that and maybe I could meet you and go from there?"

"Yeah Ben, its fine. And I appreciate that Jimmy's looking out for me. It's good to know your friends have your back. I don't really want to get into it know but, the last few months have been, well they haven't been especially great. That's how I started going to see Julie Bright and how

I ended up at the dance the other night. So I'm just starting to get out of it now. I call it the black pool Ben, cause it seems like once I fell in, it was into the deep gunky end and I keep getting pulled under by it. I'm ready to get out of it for good, but I guess it doesn't happen just because you want it to."

"No, it doesn't Willy, especially when you are dwelling on the past. From what Jimmy said, I know you were a stockbroker for a long time, apparently a very successful one, and now you are working with a media company. Is that your future? Where do you see yourself in five years?"

"That is a good question I don't have an answer to. What I hope to find now is something that really excites me. XYZmedia is a wonderful company. They do great work. But I'm really just their salesman; I don't do any of the video or web work or whatever. I just meet people and hope to open some accounts. I've got nothing against being a salesman, when I have something I am really excited about it can be a lot of fun. But the reason I quit being a stockbroker was that industry changed quite a lot. Early on I loved it because I could write my own seminars, newspaper articles, recommend stocks in companies that seemed to be on the leading edge of new industries. I spent a great deal of time with my clients, felt like I understood what their challenges were and really enjoyed offering solutions that made sense to me. Little by little, I was unable to do those things. The corporate lawyers seemed to be running the business as far as the brokers were concerned, and I was finally only able to just sell what felt like 'stuff.' The money was still potentially good, but I wanted something that made my time feel like it was being spent adding value and lit me up. That's what I want now Ben, to feel all lit up, to be excited about my life. Does that make sense?"

"Does it ever, Willy. So you got excited by getting to understand your client's needs and offering solutions. You enjoyed writing and delivering presentations. Adding your personal value to solve problems sounds like it was what it was all about for you. Is that what you are saying?"

Willy laughed. "Abe Lincoln had nothing on you, Ben. You said in three sentences what it takes me in a couple of pages. You got it."

"What you described is pretty much what I do. I believe a business that is not going forward is going backwards. Most of my clients are guys who started their business with an idea, and they still just really see that initial idea. So, nothing really changes, the business keeps doing what it's been doing and as long as the owner is making an OK living, they are happy. But if they are making money, sooner or later they are going to get competition they didn't have before. That's one scenario that comes up enough to lead to business for me. The guy is so close to the business he can't see his new opportunities. So I go in, listen, give him feedback. I'm giving them a lot of value. And if we can get in there early enough, so much the better."

"Are there some sort of guiding principles you start off with when you are beginning a new consultation, Ben?"

"That's a great question that is almost never asked. If I was to summarize them, they would begin with basic human nature. Most all of us are resistant to change. We like things just the way they are. Have you found that to be generally true?"

"Very definitely. No matter what most of my clients may have said, most of them did not like to take any risks. They liked the reward, but not the downside."

"Exactly. We keep finding the same thing. I often hear 'if it ain't broke, don't fix it.' Which sounds good, but it might mean missing the bigger picture, which is called the future. Another principle along those lines is that most people would rather be right than to be rich. Our ego has a lot to do with the decisions we make. Doing something different, to some folks anyway, seems to imply they were doing something wrong to begin with. It doesn't mean that at all, it's just that time does change things and they could be doing things better."

"I can relate to that. I was very slow to change my own business model because it was a good one for quite awhile. Everyone was happy for a long time."

"I'm sure they were. See, we are all too close to our own game, we can't really see it for what it is and, especially, what it could be. I speak from experience on that one myself."

"Is that why Tiger Woods has a coach?"

Ben laughed. "That is a very good question we should ask ten people every day, Willy. It would lead to new business. Most of the people we all meet with probably have mostly the same customers they've always had, the business seems like it's going along fine and they earn a good living, so what else is there? They quit looking for new opportunities when business got to a certain happy point. And who can blame them? They are living the dream."

"How do you help them manage their growth?"

"You ask really good questions, Willy. I encourage them to work towards having to replace themselves. What I mean by that is it seems that if we do something long enough it can get a bit stale. We lose our drive, our vision, something goes flat. If the business does well, then it is not quite the same as it was at the beginning. Plus, most business owners wear a lot of hats, they are in charge of everything. Some of those are things the owner usually doesn't care to do. Like book keeping, or sales, or fixing things. So hiring someone to take over that responsibility frees the owner to do and think about what they do enjoy doing, which was probably why they started the business to begin with. Usually, bringing in a manger can be good. Knowing your own strengths and weaknesses is a quite valuable. But then we get back to the ego thing. What I advise is to plan on rebuilding the company on a regular basis. Based on what they have learned about themselves and their customers, to imagine themselves as a new company just getting started. What would they do differently? Because if they are successful , they are going to get some competition. So, by re-imaging their business and taking action, it's good for everyone and it makes it a good business practice."

"Sounds like a good philosophy for life in general. Can't you apply those same principles towards how we might look at our lives?"

Ben greeted this question with a big smile."You better believe it. It is always ultimately about people, Willy."

"Sounds to me like you have worked with quite a few companies, Ben."

"We have indeed. Willy, let me ask you something. Early on when you were a broker, did you see yourself as a salesman or as a consultant?"

"A consultant, definitely."

"Would you like to be a consultant again?"

"Sure, I mean, it would depend on what it was, but, yes."

"Sounds to me like we definitely have plenty to discuss."

"How about you Ben? Where do see yourself in five years?"

Ben chuckled. "I need to be careful asking you questions, Willy. Retired , for sure. I can't quite see how I am exactly going to do that, though. I'm doing pretty well. But not that well. Anyway, can you come back tomorrow morning, say at 10, and we could talk some more. I may have an idea for you."

"That would be fine Ben. I'm interested in what you've said so far."

'I'll get the check today, Willy. I need to get back to the office. A client is coming over and I need to be ready for him."

33

Willy barely noticed that he was driving on his way back to Buddy and Linda's. He kept thinking about Ben, how much the guy seemed to have a life worth living; that he enjoyed what he did and how it helped his clients. There were several moments when Ben's eyes really sparkled when he spoke. Willy could partly answer Ben's question now about where he wanted to be in five years. He wanted to also have that same shine that came into his eyes, that surge of energy that came when he was excited about what he was talking about and doing, to again see the look of thankfulness he used to get from clients after a meeting had ended.

'Is Ben going to offer me a job working with him?' Willy wondered. "Could that really be what tomorrow's meeting is about?'

After settling into his work table at Buddy's, Willy did a Google search on Ben Quigley and The BenQ Company. There was a website and it included a client list that was familiar to Willy. He didn't know any of the associates listed who worked with Ben, but they all had various business backgrounds, mostly in finance or accounting. One was an attorney. It was impressive.

In his inbox, there was an email from EcotechSC, the tire recycling company he had been in contact with about doing some video work. They were interested in having a meeting. That was good and bad because he suddenly realized he'd already moved on a bit, at least in his mind, from XYZmedia. But he was glad to have something else to send over to Dan. He replied to their email and a meeting date was set for the following week. He forwarded that information to Dan Hitchens, who would be delighted to have a new customer.

Liz had emailed as well. Just to say she was thinking about him and couldn't wait to see him later that evening.

"Holy Smokeronees!" was all Willy could say. What a day he was having. And then he suddenly felt the pull of the black pool. It would all go to hell, faster than he could imagine. Liz would dump him, Ben wasn't going to offer him a job and the EcotechSC thing would turn into a very long and slow No. Why would all this turn out any different than the way everything else always seemed to?

He lay down on the bed, not even his own bed, his friend's bed. Willy sunk even deeper into despair. 'Why do I have to be me? What did I ever do that was so bad?'

And then something Julie had said more than once came into his mind. That when these thoughts came up, overwhelming him, he should know that those messages are not true, they were lies originating from the depths of the dark pool, that it was the depression speaking. He shouldn't give in to it.

He got off the bed and left the room. He needed to get outside for a minute, even if it was hot; just to get away and breathe in some real air, feel the sunshine, touch base with nature, get grounded in reality. Yeah, life sucked some times. But only some times. Life was actually pretty great. It just took moments like he had just had to be reminded, to know the difference.

34

Arriving early the following day for his meeting with Ben, Willy was a bit surprised at how energized he felt. He was a night person by nature, rarely going to bed before 1AM. The night before, as he was thinking about this meeting, several ideas had suddenly come to him and he had sat at his desk making notes on action steps that could be taken for what he had envisioned.

"Good morning, Sheila, how are you doing?"

"Hi Mr. O'Shea, it is nice to see you again. I'll let Ben know you are here. Can I get you some coffee or anything while you are waiting?"

"Thanks, no I'm fine."

The wait was a short one.

"Morning, Ben, good to see you."

"You too, Willy. I was just going to get some coffee. Would you care to join me?"

"Sure thing."

They walked back through the reception area to a kitchen down the other hallway. There was a round wooden table with chairs for six people, a microwave oven next to the refrigerator, a bottled water cooler, and an impressive coffee maker.

"This is where we have our company meetings. Have a seat, Willy. How do you like your coffee?"

"Cream and sugar is perfect, thanks. So how many people are working here, Ben?"

"Counting Sheila, there are six of us," explained Ben as he sat across from Willy." Some work from home, which is fine, but throughout the day everyone comes to the office at some point. We plan to get together once a week so we can all be across the table from one another. It's a good group, they all have their specialties and, often enough, several of them are working together on some of our accounts."

"Have they been with you for long?"

"Yes, John Wilson has been here the longest, about eight years. Rosie Jones has been here for nearly the same. Jim Davis and Joe Lucciano have each been with us for about three years. Willy, I have been thinking about meeting you yesterday, what I knew about you from Jimmy, and then I made a few calls to some other people who have known you too. They all said pretty much the same thing. It matched the impression I had. The bottom line is, would you consider some sort of affiliation with my company? Maybe work here full time? Does that have any interest for you, based on the very little you know about what we do here."

"Ben, I enjoyed speaking with you very much yesterday. I also did some research on you and the company after I left. My gut feeling is that I would love to work here. You asked me a good question yesterday, when you asked if I wanted to be a consultant. That is a big yes. I have had a nice relationship with Dan especially, at XYZmedia, but I am ready to move on. What did you have in mind in terms of what I would do?"

"You seem to have a lot of experience in sales and marketing. Most of our clients are weak in those areas. They have salesmen, they have websites and all, but they aren't getting a lot of return on their investments in those areas. I was thinking that would be a starting point and see how it goes. What I would most like would be you working here full time. I can pay you a salary, not a big one, but $3000 a month, let's say for the next six months and then look at the compensation again after that. You would have an office on this floor. We have parking out back and you'd have your own space. What we don't have is medical or a 401K, maybe one day, but not in the foreseeable future. So, that's the offer. What do you say?"

"I say yes. I have a few things I am finishing up for Dan, which I am sure you understand."

"Definitely. That is great, Willy! You have your own hours, there is no time clock, but I would like us to spend most of our days together for the next couple of weeks. Give us a chance to brainstorm, meet some clients together. When can you start?"

"How about right now?"

Ben's smile couldn't have been bigger. He stood, as did Willy, and they shook hands.

"Welcome aboard, Willy O'Shea. I think this is the beginning of a beautiful friendship."

"Thanks Ben, but you stole that line."

"My compliments to the writers of Casablanca. Do you have any questions, thoughts or ideas, before we get Sheila started on ordering business cards, get you keys and show you your office. It has a new computer, by the way."

"I have a few thoughts, for sure. The questions will come later. You said that you aren't very good at marketing the firm. How would you feel about me taking that on?"

"That would be very good. Do you have an idea how you would do that right off the bat?"

"Yes, I worked on this a bit last night. My first idea is to get in front of trade association meetings and give a presentation entitled "Why does Tiger Woods have a coach?" The premise being that he is so close to his golf game, that even the worlds greatest needs a consultant, a coach to show him what he could be doing even better. I was wondering about a weekly or monthly eNewsletter to all your clients and prospective clients, discussing some basic ideas as a way of staying in contact. A nice touch for that would be a short video attached to it of you, or John, Rosie, Jim or Joe, discussing something briefly that should be of interest. What is your reaction to those ideas?"

"Other than being afraid I would break the camera, those sound like pretty amazingly good ideas. You can do that?"

"Sure."

"Well then, yes. Let's talk some more about that later, but yes."

"I also have an idea for who might be my first prospective client. Are you familiar with AmSouth Distributors?"

"Heard of them, don't know them. Aren't they out on the Interstate somewhere?"

Willy nodded. "They have just signed an agreement with XYZmedia for video work about a new product. The owner is Ed Shields and he offered me a job in sales. Ed said his salespeople aren't producing what he hoped for. So I was thinking last night that he needs some consulting and that we should call on him about that and who knows what else."

"You've been here thirty minutes, have given me some solid marketing ideas and have a prospective client. Wow. Yes, we can go see Ed Shields, when you think the time is right. Now, let's get you situated here. Oh, we don't have any kind of dress code, in case you were wondering. You are a professional. Some days I look like I am going to the beach, other days I am wearing a suit, most days somewhere in between. Ready to get started, Willy?"

"Let's do it."

"Upstairs, I have some rooms for me to get away to from time to time. You may not know this but this was where I worked and lived for a long time, before I met Michele and moved to her house on Sullivan's Island, but we stay here sometimes."

35

Willy thought about cancelling his appointment with Julie scheduled for later that afternoon. He felt so good about his life all of a sudden, as if the huge boulder he had been pushing uphill all these difficult years had reached the top and now was racing downhill with him on top of it. He was eager to get the work with The Ben Q Company underway. Out of respect for Julie and for all of the time and good advice she had given him, cancelling would have been rude and disrespectful, so he arrived early.

As he waited in the reception area, he found a book on her bookshelf he hadn't noticed there before. It was called 'Bird by Bird,' written by Anne Lamott. He wasn't familiar with that book so he began leafing through it. A particular phrase caught his eye, which was where the title of the book came from. Her father had once apparently given some advice to her brother, who was feeling overwhelmed by a school assignment about every type of bird. The advice was to do the assignment 'one bird at a time.' On the drive over, Willy had been furiously writing down notes on all the different ideas he had, all the different people he might call, and wondering how to get it all done at once. It was the perfect advice for him at exactly the right moment.

"Which book are you looking at, Willy?" Julie asked quietly as she entered the lobby.

"Bird by Bird', have you read it?"

"That might be just the book for you to read now. It seems we often find just the right books, people or ideas at the right time. You can borrow it if you would like. Come on in."

After getting settled in her session room, Julie asked how life was going for Willy these past few days.

"Julie, it has been, well, amazing doesn't quite describe it. Ben Quigley and I have gotten together several times and he has offered and I have accepted a job working with him. Liz Oakes and I are in a relationship. I feel very excited. In fact, I was up quite late, even for me, writing down ideas. The boys will be home next week and I can't wait to see them. Life feels pretty darn good today."

"There was a light in your face when I saw you in the reception area that I haven't seen in a long time. I am so happy for you, Willy. What will be different about working with Ben then say, what you do for XYZ or when you were a stockbroker?"

"The idea is I will be doing more consulting and less selling, just like in the earlier days when I was a broker?"

"So, a shift?"

"Shift happens. Holy cow Julie that is exactly what this is. Omigosh! I hadn't quite seen it that way, I just felt it."

Julie laughed. "You see what happens when you create a true and right intention for yourself? You knew what you wanted. And the opportunity for it to manifest itself arrived. But you made it happen, Willy. It didn't just show up on your doorstep. You remember what that voice of yours said? 'You already have everything you need.' It was all there inside you all along, and you listened to the voice. You, Willy, took the action steps to get right where you are this moment. You heard your true self, Willy. A shift happened. There will be others."

Willy was blown away by this. He had been so close to himself that he couldn't quite see what was happening.

"Do you remember what you did after those awful moments in your car? You took a step away from your house, from that life you had been living that was literally killing you. You took a very big step into the darkest of nights, totally into the unknown. You just could not be where you were for even another moment. You didn't know where you were going. But you took the first step. All you could look for was the next step. In life, we often become so concerned with looking for all the steps and the perfect ending, that we don't spend enough time noticing where we are right now and what is the next little step we need to take that gets us going on a new path. You have been taking lots of bigger steps every day since. It's not very different than what she wrote about in 'Bird by Bird.' Do you find it remarkable that book caught your eye out of the hundreds we have out there? It's been sitting there since long before you came in here that first day."

"So part of the shift is seeing things differently. That makes sense, although it seems a bit woo-woo to me."

Julie laughed again. "Some of that is woo-woo and most of it isn't. Living a life is not an exact science. You can't just write down what's going to happen and it does. We do our best, we prepare as much as we can and then we have to let go of the outcomes, just see what happened and learn something from it."

"Sounds like a plan."

"So, I need to say something now that is not intended to be a downer. Are you familiar with the George Harrison song "Beware of Darkness?"

"Probably, I've always loved his music."

"Find it after you leave, search on Pandora or YouTube. Listen to it. I want you to remember that the black pool, as you call it, is always lurking. As good as you feel right now, there will be lots of ups and downs ahead for you. That's a good thing to know. But for the moment, I have an assignment for you. I want you to go have fun tonight. Just celebrate what you have done here, Willy. You did this work that got you to where Ben and Liz want you in their lives. Your sons are going to be thrilled to see you. So, get out of here. I will see you same time next week here and at The Pathfinders tomorrow night. Don't forget to take 'Bird by Bird with you. You always said you liked to write. That book is about how to be a writer. I suspect you may start doing some now."

"Did you know that Liz is a book editor?"

Smiling, Julie shook her head. "Woo woo, Willy." They both laughed.

"That doesn't surprise me at all. Now, get out of here. See you tomorrow night."

36

Several mornings later, Willy was back in Ed Shields office.

"So, tell me what you wanted to come see me about, Willy. I was a little surprised when you said you were no longer solely representing XYZmedia. I had a good meeting with Dan, by the way. He was very complementary about you and said this is all good between you and him. What did you have in mind?"

"Ed, during our meetings here, you mentioned several times that you were disappointed in the results your sales team is delivering. You were kind enough to offer me a position in hopes that not only could I help more sales, but also to perhaps be of some value in assisting your current team to sell more as well. Is that still a major priority for you?"

"Is it ever! Have you changed your mind about coming to work here?" Ed asked eagerly.

"Not exactly. What I can do might be just as helpful to you, and it might save you some money at the same time."

"Alright, how could you do that?"

"Very simply, I could spend some time here with your sales people, listen to them make appointments, perhaps go with them on some sales calls, attend a few sales meetings.

After which, I should be able to help them do things differently, improve your sales process and get them better organized as a team. You mentioned, for example, that they all thoroughly understood the products and could talk anyone's ear off about what they did and how they worked, even how they were made. But selling is much more than that. I can help you get the results you want, and at a lower cost than what you were going to pay me as a salary. How does that sound to you?"

"Why don't I just send them to Dale Carnegie or something?"

"That is undoubtedly one of the suggestions I will make. Dale Carnegie is a great organization. But your sales people may simply need to shift the way they are approaching and speaking with their clients. That would be the first step. Get them as prepared as possible, in front of as many prospects as possible and then we can study the results. Then, Dale Carnegie might have an even bigger impact on their work and get you an even higher return on your investment there. They will be the same people, but I will help them shift their approach and hopefully, produce much higher results. Does that sound like what you want?"

"It is. I've always liked your style Willy. When could you get started on this? How much is it going to cost?"

"The next step would be for me to meet some of your people and attend a sales meeting. Then, my colleague Ben Quigley and I will return with a detailed proposal. When is your next sales meeting?"

"It will be next Monday at 10AM. Alright, why don't you be there? I will be sure you can speak with some of them afterward. I will be glad to meet with Ben Quigley. I know him by reputation only. My friend Charlie Allen mentioned to me once how helpful Ben was to him."

"I'll be here Monday then. It should take just a few days to collect my thoughts and create an action plan for you. What if Ben and I meet with you next Thursday, say at 11AM to get started?"

"That would be fine, Willy. I am truly excited about this. I knew you could help us. I just didn't expect it to be this way."

"Outcomes often arrive in a different way than we would guess. See you Monday, Ed."

37

"Yes! Yes! Yes!" Willy shouted as he closed his car door. He pounded joyously on his steering wheel, as he bounced up and down in his seat, just like he probably did when he was just a child opening Christmas presents. "It can happen. It is happening, Omigosh! "

And so Willy O'Shea was very excited as he drove the Honda out of the Am South parking lot. He turned back towards Charleston. The sun was high in the sky before him, casting bright sunbeams through some clouds. Willy thought about some of the other calls he would make after arriving at The Ben Q Company and talking with Ben.

His thoughts shifted. He imagined Liz and how much he looked forward to seeing her later that afternoon. He thought about Marcie and how thankful he was that she was his daughter. He was especially excited to think about his sons. Johnny and Billy would be home tomorrow, and he couldn't wait to see them.

The Voice spoke. "You already have everything you need. Keep your mind on your work and everything will be OK."

"You better believe it," Willy replied.

As the sun burst through the clouds, Willy felt the light he had been searching for surging. It was right there where it had always been, deep inside of him. He entered the highway, headed for Charleston and all that lay before him.